IMPOSTERS IN PARADISE

An utterly gripping romantic suspense mystery page-turner

FAITH MARTIN

writing as

MAXINE BARRY

JOFFE BOOKS

Revised edition 2021
Joffe Books, London
www.joffebooks.com

First published in Great Britain in 2002

Cover art by Jarmila Takač

ISBN: 978-1-78931-788-6

ONE

New York

JFK Airport was huge, noisy and just a bit frightening for novices, so Imogen Dacres was glad that she'd got her connecting flight sorted out quickly. Now she could relax with a much-needed cup of coffee, since the flight out from Heathrow had left her feeling like a limp lettuce leaf.

Not that she looked like one, and many pairs of appreciative male eyes watched her progress through the self-service cafeteria. But at twenty-five she was now used to such glances, and knew exactly how meaningless and empty they were.

She paid for her coffee with her newly changed, unfamiliar currency, and as she folded her slender five-foot ten-inch frame into a moulded plastic chair she sighed heavily.

Her waist-length, dead-straight black hair was plaited and looped around her head in an elegant style that was good for everyday wear. It certainly suited her work environment as a secretary at St Bede's College in Oxford. This contrasted with her pale skin, which, combined with big, deep-blue eyes inherited from an Irish grandfather, made Imogen easily the most striking woman in the place.

She raised the cup of coffee to her lips and took a sip, surprised at the superior quality of it. For a modern woman of the brave new millennium, she felt a little absurd that this should be her first trip abroad. But while her friends could afford package holidays in the sun, all of Imogen's less-than-generous wages had been spent on looking after her mother, Rebecca, an invalid of many years.

Rebecca had married the handsome but intrinsically lazy Geoff Dacres when she'd been only twenty-one. Two children, a boy and a girl, had quickly followed, but by then Rebecca had grown resentful of her husband's jobless, lack-adaisical way of living.

Things came to a crisis when she became ill with an incurable wasting disease, and Geoff, being Geoff, had quickly deserted the sinking ship, taking only his son Robbie with him. Rebecca had fought him for custody, of course, but had had too much stacked against her. Geoff Dacres came from fairly affluent, middle-class parents, who'd promptly provided him with a first-class lawyer, and Rebecca, sensing that she might just lose her daughter to the Dacre family as well, had reluctantly knuckled under and agreed to the generous visitation rights on offer. She then moved herself and Imogen to a small, more affordable council house in the large village of Kidlington, a near-suburb of Oxford.

With Rebecca's illness meaning she could no longer work, Imogen had left school at the earliest opportunity and taken the first job she was offered as a junior in one of Oxford's many colleges. Now, nine years later, she'd risen in rank to senior secretary/PA to the bursar of St Bede's.

Realising that her coffee, so different from the cheap instant she was used to, was cooling, Imogen took another sip. Many things, she mused, would be different now.

She'd taken a month's leave from the college and was on her way to Bermuda. To Bermuda! As a young girl, she'd often dreamed of visiting a romantic desert island, with palm trees, blue seas and warm tropical breezes. And now that she was actually on her way, with the fabled Bermuda Triangle to add to the thrill of excitement, she knew she should be elated. But, of course, she wasn't. Not under the circumstances.

With a start she heard the number of her flight being called, and quickly made her way to the gate. She was wearing her best travelling suit, which hugged her hips and shoulders in a tight but comfortable embrace and showed off her elegant shape to perfection.

The plane she boarded was much smaller than the one she'd flown in from Heathrow – it looked to seat about 100 passengers – and she was surprised by how empty it was. She took her seat and instantly buckled her belt. As she waited for take-off, she read the blurb and learned that it would take about two hours to reach Bermuda's main international airport at Kindley Field.

She'd thoroughly researched the mysterious island of Bermuda before coming, of course. It was vitally important that she be prepared. After all, she had no idea what might be waiting for her once she landed.

'At last.' The soft voice came from the woman who'd been shown into the seat next to hers a scant two minutes ago. 'I hate waiting around for planes to take off, don't you?'

Imogen turned to look at her and smiled vaguely. From her upper-class accent she was obviously English as well, and had long dark hair which fell over her shoulders in untidy waves. Her eyes were wide, slightly myopic-looking, and deeply brown.

'I haven't done much flying,' Imogen admitted.

'Oh, I hate it. And I heard on the radio that there's a storm raging over Bermuda at the moment. Great, huh?'

Wonderful, Imogen thought with a wry twist of her lips. Just what she needed to hear. Then the plane was powering down the runway, and there was that stomach-lurching moment as they left the ground. Slowly, Imogen began to relax. The plane climbed easily and levelled off. The stewardesses came around, Imogen refusing anything alcoholic, her travelling companion treating herself to a double Martini.

Her body insisted that it must getting on towards evening, but with the time difference she knew that wasn't right. So this is jet lag, Imogen thought wearily, and smiled. Perhaps she might doze for a little while. Just at that moment the plane hit an air pocket and seemed to drop like a stone, and both women made a grab for the arms of their seats. On the other hand, Imogen thought wryly, forget the dozing.

The captain's voice came over the speaker, relaying the rather dismaying information that they were indeed heading for stormy weather and that they might experience a bit of turbulence. He finished with the anti-climatic announcement that in Hamilton it was raining cats and dogs. So much for her vision of a sun-drenched tropical island!

'Have you been to Bermuda before?' her companion asked, obviously not the kind who liked to sit quietly and pretend her neighbour didn't exist, and Imogen, not sure whether to be relieved or not, smiled and shook her head.

'No. You?'

The woman also shook her head. She looked to be about Imogen's age, and when she reached up to brush a strand of hair off her cheek Imogen noticed the bracelet she was wearing. Made of gold, it had either white-gold or platinum daisies making up the chain that linked onto a long, solid yellow-gold bar. On it, she could see that some letters had been engraved, beginning with a capital I – her own initial. The woman saw her glance, and smiled, holding out her wrist and turning the distinctive-looking bracelet so that she could read it. Isadora.

'That's me. What on earth my mother was thinking when she called me that I don't know. Everyone calls me Izzie. Isadora Van Harte,' she said, thrusting her hand out.

'Imogen Dacres,' she returned, taking the other woman's hand with a grin.

The plane hit another air pocket.

'I need another drink,' Isadora said in a rush and raised her hand for the stewardess. 'I hate flying in bad weather. By the time we get to Bermuda, I want to be thoroughly blotto.

Cheers.' She raised the glass she'd just been served and took a deep draught.

Imogen sipped at her lemonade. Her father had drunk more than was good for him, and her mother, due to her ill health, had never been permitted to drink at all. Not surprisingly then, Imogen, having grown up in a teetotal house, had never acquired the drinking habit either.

'Are you going to Bermuda on holiday?' she asked Isadora, who shook her head.

'Not exactly. I'm coming over to heal a family rift,' her words were ever so slightly slurred. 'My mother died a year ago, my father long before that, and then just last month I got a phone call from this aunt I never even knew I had. Apparently there was some kind of family bust-up,' she shrugged. 'Anyway, my aunt, Elizabeth, invited me over, and since I hadn't got anything better to do . . .'

Imogen nodded. 'I lost my mother recently too,' she said quietly. 'She'd been ill for a long time . . .' her voice trailed off and she glanced out of her window, and then promptly wished she hadn't. Pale grey clouds were darkening to an ominous slate grey, and she felt her first real twinge of anxiety. She turned her gaze resolutely away from the sky and back to Isadora. 'Know much about the place? Bermuda, I mean?' she asked, deliberately lightening the mood.

Isadora laughed. 'Not a thing,' she said, with charming self-effacement. 'Apart from the fact that planes and boats are always disappearing into the triangle.'

Imogen laughed and shuddered. 'Don't. Do you want me to tell you about it? I'm afraid I'm one of those annoying people who always have to know about the places they visit.' Not true, of course, but she had no intention of telling anybody the real reason she was going to Bermuda, and why it was so important that she kept her wits about her.

The plane hit yet another air pocket and the lights flickered. Both women paled.

'Hell yes,' Isadora yelped. 'Tell me everything! Please! Anything to take my mind off *this*.'

And so Imogen launched into a speech, sounding a bit like a tour guide, but it kept both their minds off the weather outside.

Bermuda, Imogen explained, was some 21 square miles long, made up of 181 named low-lying coral islands and islets, of which only twenty were inhabited. The largest island was Bermuda, then St George's and St David's, which were among the seven islands linked by causeways and bridges.

Isadora listened to all this with the determined attention of a girl in a school room. Resolutely ignoring the now unmistakable lurching of the plane, Imogen ploughed on, giving a brief history of the place, from its discovery by the Spanish mariner Juan de Bermúdez in the early sixteenth century, to its life as a penal settlement until 1862, and then the political unrest and the assassination of the Governor General in 1973.

At this point, the captain's voice came over the speaker again, asking them to fasten their seat belts for the time being. This the two women did with much alacrity, Imogen glancing anxiously at her watch as she did so. 'Only thirty minutes to go before we land,' she said, with obvious relief.

'Right,' Isadora said with false brightness. 'So, what takes you to Bermuda? From the sound of it you could take up a teaching post there! But I suppose you're on holiday?'

Imogen felt her face stiffen, and she forced herself to smile. 'That's right,' she lied. 'Holiday.' And her hand clutched tightly around her handbag.

As Isadora raised her hand to appeal for yet another drink, Imogen took the opportunity to open her handbag and extract her brother's letter. She already knew it off by heart, but the mention of her 'holiday' to Bermuda made her want to read it again. But just then Isadora, having been told that they couldn't serve drinks while the 'Fasten Seat Belts' sign was on, turned back to her, and Imogen hastily thrust the letter into the deep pocket of her jacket.

'So much for being blotto,' Isadora muttered grimly.

Imogen sighed. It wasn't often that her brother Robbie wrote to her. Having grown up under the twin influences of his well-to-do grandparents and his good-time father, it was hardly surprising that her brother had little in common with her. It had been par for the course that Robbie had back-packed around the world, finally washing up in Bermuda. There, so his letter had informed her, he'd found a job working as an instructor at a diving school.

During their childhood years, they'd often met up for seaside holidays with one parent or the other, and if they weren't close, they at least liked each other. Robbie had inherited their father's charm and easy-going generosity, and his few letters to her over the years had been filled with the same take-it-or-leave-it gaiety. But this last letter had been different. It had started off all right, with Robbie's usual inconsequential chatter about the beach bars, and the way the tourists gave him a headache (none of them could dive worth a damn), but soon the letter became very un-Robbie-like indeed. She'd also noticed that it had been written with two different pens, one in pale blue ink and one in dark blue; the majority of the writing was in the pale blue, but many other words were picked out in dark blue. She just couldn't understand why. However, the contents of the letter were clear enough. He was worried, he said, about his boss. There was something 'rotten in the State of Bermuda', a misquote from *Hamlet* which was typical of him. At first she'd just put it down to his usual vivid imagination.

But then tragedy had struck, and her suspicions had been instantly aroused because it just wasn't—

The plane gave a massive lurch, the lights went out for a second, then flickered back on again. Their few fellow passengers began to whisper tensely to each other.

'That's it,' Isadora said thickly. 'If it does that again, I'm not going to be held responsible for my actions!'

Imogen's own heart was beating hard in what felt like the base of her throat, and she took several long, deep breaths. Her twenty or so fellow passengers were also stirring uneasily. Once again the captain's voice came over the speakers, assuring them that they were all but through the worst, and would be touching down in Bermuda in fifteen minutes.

It cheered everyone up, although the plane continued to buck alarmingly. Beside her, Isadora began to fidget strenuously with her bracelet. Imogen guessed that it was a nervous habit she had, and wasn't at all surprised when, a few moments later, the catch on the bracelet came open and the pretty gold band slithered down onto Isadora's lap.

'Oh damn,' she muttered, picking it up and looping it back around her wrist, her elbow jutting out as she tried awkwardly to fasten it again. Never an easy thing to do one-handed. After several tries, she sighed heavily. It didn't help that her hands were shaking.

'Here, let me,' Imogen offered, leaning over and holding the two ends together. But the locking mechanism was one she'd never seen before, and it totally defeated her.

'No, you push that little bit up, then under,' Isadora said, beginning to giggle. Imogen had to laugh too. She knew it was a result of their nerves, but the two women, heads together, found themselves giggling like schoolchildren as Imogen failed again and again to get the clasp to work. Eventually Isadora shook her head. 'Look, I tell you what. Hold out your own wrist, and I'll fasten the clasp, and you watch how it's done.'

'Deal,' Imogen said drolly. But the bit of nonsense had passed five minutes away. Surely they couldn't be far off from landing now? She blinked as a blue streak of lightning zigzagged outside her window and momentarily blinded her. Several passengers yelped as they too were dazzled.

Imogen half-turned in her seat, her back to the window, while Isadora took one end of the clasp, threaded it through the hollow loop at the other end and then, in an upside-down gesture, turned it back on itself and fastened it, the clasp pressing firmly into the skin of Imogen's inner wrist.

'Well no wonder I couldn't get it done up,' Imogen huffed in feigned exasperation, and reached forward to—

There was another sudden and impossibly vivid flash of blue. Then a strange fizzling, crunching sound. All the lights went out and stayed out. Several women screamed. Beside her, she felt Isadora's hand grab her own, clasping so hard it made her bones ache. Even with the lights out, and the sky only a stormy dark curtain outside, there was still enough light in the cabin to see one of the stewardesses go forward into the cockpit.

For what felt like a long while, but couldn't have been more than a minute, the aeroplane was awash with terrified, babbling voices. Perhaps that's why it took so long for Imogen to realise that instead of sitting levelly in her seat, her whole body was angling forward. And leaning forward at an increasingly steep angle. It took her another few seconds to realise that the plane had now gone unnaturally quiet.

At first she thought it was because, after the initial surprise, her fellow passengers, like herself, had all gone quiet. Then she realised it was more than that. The silence was deeper, far more ominous than just the absence of human voices.

She couldn't hear the engines! Which meant that they had no power. They were going down!

As if on cue, everyone began to scream.

TWO

This can't be happening, Imogen thought. It just can't. Perhaps the pilot was deliberately losing altitude. They might be coming in to land. But no matter how desperately she wanted to cling on to this comforting thought, she simply couldn't. Because now she was leaning so far forward, her forehead was almost touching the seat in front of her.

Too steep, she thought, too steep. The words, once ensconced in her mind, seemed to echo around her head, plunging her into the deep, dark, cavern-like place called terror. Dimly she heard a stewardess shouting out instructions. 'Put your head between your knees. *Brace, brace, brace.*'

Beside her, she could hear Isadora Van Harte crying, great choking, despairing sobs, and somewhere in the rear, a woman was screaming constantly. Imogen could hear nothing else but those two sounds overlaid by the thundering of her own heart.

The iron-hot taste of fear was rank and sickening in her throat and on her tongue. Her head was spinning, her knuckles deathly white where she was clutching the ends of the seat's arm rests.

How much longer, she wondered despairingly. It already felt like years since the lights had gone out. How high could they possibly have been? Surely they'd land soon.

She heard someone laughing hysterically, and with a start of shame and surprise realised that it was her. *Shut up*, she told herself furiously, her eyes staring down at her shoes and the small patch of carpet she could see underneath them. *You sound so stupid, laughing like a hyena.*

It was her last thought before the plane seemed to give a gigantic backwards lunge; her head whiplashed back and then forward again in a sickening jerk, knocking her forehead on the seat in front and sending her far, far away.

And yet, she was still somewhere where she was vaguely aware of the sound of tearing, rending metal. And then she felt the sudden rush of something cold and alien. A weird kind of freedom. What . . . ?

Dizzily, Imogen opened her eyes. Her seat was moving around so strangely, it was as if it was gliding her across the room. And her feet were cold. Bemused, she looked down, but instead of seeing her shoes and the patch of beige carpet that had become so ingrained in her memory, she saw only swirling water. A sweet wrapper floated past her shin, tickling it.

Water. They were in the sea.

Get your seat belt off. At once. This cold, logical thought suddenly came into her head like a real voice, as if she were hearing someone else commentating. It was impersonal, sounding directly from inside her skull. Without realising it, her hands fumbled for her belt and felt suddenly cold. She glanced down and saw that the water was now at her waist – and rising. The plane was sinking.

Why could she hear no one else? Shouldn't men be cursing or calling for their wives or partners? Surely a stewardess should be yelling out orders to evacuate or whatever.

Her head felt so fuzzy. She turned to Isadora to tell her to take off her seat belt too. But Isadora wasn't there. She laughed again. Now where had that woman got to?

Take off your seat belt. There was that voice again, still cold and impersonal, but more demanding now.

'All right, all right,' Imogen muttered, getting free and floating away from her seat. She found herself swimming in a sea of jagged metal, floating luggage and . . . Her eyes widened. Someone was coming towards her, not swimming in a sort of doggy paddle half-remembered from schooldays as she was, but floating face down.

He's dead. The voice again. *Swim towards the jagged hole over to your left.*

Imogen obediently turned and felt something bump her head. The ceiling. She'd floated all the way to the top, but how could that be when they were sinking?

She was going to drown!

Soon the air bubble was going to be gone, and then . . . Sea water washed over her face and into her mouth, and she tasted salt. She should pray, shouldn't she? She gave a gurgling yip as seawater lashed over her eyes, making them smart, and she closed them instinctively.

Open your eyes. The voice again. There was something so hypnotic about it that Imogen found herself following the instruction. The pain was brief and fierce, but then she was in a swirling underwater world, her distorted vision just good enough for her to see where she was going.

Her chest was beginning to hurt. *Swim through the jagged hole. Careful not to tear yourself on the metal.*

This voice certainly is bossy, Imogen thought. Nevertheless she obeyed it, propelling herself forward, using the still-anchored seats to push her way through the plane and out into the big blue sea.

Up, the voice said. *See the light?*

Imogen looked up, and through the dense, painful water, she could indeed see light. She went up, not really sure how she was doing it, but her body was naturally buoyant. Her chest really was hurting now.

Suddenly, her eyes were seeing brighter, whiter blue. Her vision, previously distorted, became clear again. But she could hold her breath no longer. She opened her mouth. Air rushed in. Air? Not water? What was going on? The guiding voice was silent now.

Later, of course, she would understand that the voice had been her own subconscious mind cutting through the panic and confusion of concussion and fear, leading her from the plane. But for now she was content just to float, to let the water take her, to look up at the sky above her and breathe.

She didn't look around her. She didn't want to look. She knew, in some deep dark part of her that was now stubbornly silent, that she would only see bits of the plane and more floating bodies. No. She didn't want to think about that.

Sharks. Now why had she thought of sharks? She raised a hand to her head and promptly sank. Water was suddenly everywhere. She resurfaced and coughed, then lay back again, just letting herself float.

Shouldn't she be doing something? Survivors were supposed to swim for pieces of wreckage and cling on, weren't they? But that would require so much effort. She was happy just floating. The sea didn't seem to mind her just floating along.

But after a few moments, she summoned her last shred of energy to grab onto the piece of sheet metal that was her nearest life raft. With an exhausted sigh she flung her arms over it, and closed her eyes.

Time that she was unaware of passed, as time always does.

What on earth was that racket? Imogen opened her sore eyes. A strange, loud, clackety-clacking was making her head throb. For the first time she became aware of a headache.

And then she saw it – coming towards her across the sky – a giant red and white dragonfly. It must be a Bermudan dragonfly, she thought with a smile. They didn't have dragonflies that big in England. So big a man could ride on it.

Imogen frowned. A man. Leaning out, looking down. With a big white head; a big, bulbous white head. Like an insect within an insect. Silly, it's a crash helmet, she realised with a giggle. And then the voice came back – cold and bossy as ever.

Wave, it said.

Wave?

Wave, it repeated firmly, so Imogen idly lifted a hand and waved. Another giggle. Her throat was so sore. She could do with a nice cup of tea.

The man with the crash helmet began gesturing to the man in front. Pointing down at her. Now that was rude.

Imogen felt tired. She wanted to go back to sleep. So she did.

Someone was talking. Voices again, but this time not a strange voice inside her head, but warm, normal, vibrant voices not far away. Women talking. Gossiping. Something about Julie's latest ex. She drifted off. Came back again. The voices were still talking. But she couldn't quite get her eyes to open. It felt as if someone had sneaked in and superglued them together.

Robbie. An image of her brother suddenly broke into her mind. Robbie, laughing, suntanned, fit and fickle. Robbie. Dead. So mysteriously and suspiciously dead.

And suddenly, everything came back. The reason she was in Bermuda. The plane crash. Everything. Now she didn't want to open her eyes. The memories flooded through her, threatening to engulf her.

'I do hope Mrs Van Harte is all right out there,' one female voice said to the other. 'She's looking very pale.'

'Angina,' the other voice said knowingly. 'Don't worry. Dr Felixstone is keeping an eye on her. But it's just as well her niece survived. I think it might have killed her if she'd found out she was dead.'

Van Harte. Imogen frowned. She'd heard that name before somewhere. And then she remembered. Isadora, of the double Martinis, and an aunt she was going to meet for the first time in Bermuda.

'At least the plane wasn't full, that's one good thing,' the first female voice spoke up again.

'Yes, but even so. Just one survivor.'

'The Van Harte luck again,' the other one agreed.

Imogen felt herself smile. So Isadora had made it! Wonderful. Then her head began to hurt all over again. Hurt because it was buzzing, trying to tell her something. But what?

She wished she didn't have to think, but her brain was insistent – and finally came up with the answer. *Only one survivor.* But if Isadora was alive, then she herself must be dead. No. That's not right, her brain insisted. But she was tired. She couldn't be bothered to work it out. Perhaps she'd just misheard them.

She slept. And woke again. How long had she been asleep? Not long, for the same female voices were still talking. Only they sounded angrier now.

'Just who do those guys think they are? Matron keeps telling them, no one gets to see the patient except family.'

'Perhaps they're relatives of this Dacres woman they keep asking about.'

At that Imogen's eyes shot open. Dacres. She was Imogen Dacres. But who could possibly be asking after her? Nobody knew she was here. She deliberately hadn't told any of her friends where she was going, or why. It would have sounded so stupid. So melodramatic. Listen, Sue, Patty, I'm going to Bermuda because I think someone murdered my brother. It was hardly something you could say in the staff room of the quaint, genteel St Bede's College of Oxford.

But Robbie had always been too good a swimmer, too good a diver, too good an all-round athlete to make a mistake and drown the way they say he did.

'Something rotten in the State of Bermuda' indeed. That was why she'd come. To expose this rottenness, whatever it was, and find the truth.

'I daresay they've gone by now. Matron has all the charm of a snake when people try to upset the routine of the ward.'

'Not them, they're still out there in reception. Mind you, the taller one's quite a dish.'

Imogen, who had been staring at blank white ceiling tiles for some moments now, slewed her eyes around and found herself looking at two pale-blue-clad women. Nurses. She must be in hospital.

And someone outside wanted to see an Imogen Dacres. Someone who shouldn't know that she was even here.

Someone who'd killed Robbie, perhaps?

If only her head didn't ache so. She needed it clear to think things out properly. She shifted restlessly, and the movement attracted the notice of one of the nurses.

'Well, hello there,' she said softly, hurrying over and pushing a button beside the bed. 'How are you feeling?'

Imogen sighed. 'All right,' she said. But all that came out was a weak croak.

'That's the salt water,' the other nurse said sympathetically, joining her friend at the bedside. 'Your throat is very sore, I know. Do you want a sip of water?' And when Imogen nodded, the older nurse gently lifted her head and placed a plastic cup to her lips.

'Only little sips now.'

Imogen drank, wincing at the pain in her throat, suddenly realising how thirsty she'd been.

The door opened and a man walked in, dressed in a long white coat. He had gingery hair and grey eyes. 'So, you're awake at last.' He smiled down at her, his fingers reaching for her pulse. Next he took out a small torch and shone it in her eyes. 'Do you have a headache?' he asked mildly.

'Yes.'

'Do you feel sick, giddy or disorientated?'

'No.'

'Splendid. You have a mild concussion and some nasty bruises, but other than that you've been remarkably lucky,' he informed her cheerfully. 'All being well, you should be able to leave tomorrow.'

In truth she felt anything but lucky. Survivor's guilt, like a black cloud, seemed to press her back into the bed. The whole situation was still too painful to contemplate, and to take her mind off it she slowly allowed her eyes to travel around the room – the pale green and cream walls, the huge bunches of flowers, the television set up high in one corner.

Something was off, but it took her a few seconds to figure out what it was. Who had sent her the flowers? Who was there left, now that Robbie and her mother were dead, to care whether she lived or died?

'Lovely flowers, aren't they?' The older nurse saw her staring in puzzlement at the display of exotic blooms. 'The islands are a horticulturist's paradise. It's all this warm, constant weather and mild winters. They're from your aunt's own gardens.'

'Aunt?' Imogen croaked.

'Yes. Mrs Van Harte. She's waiting to see you.' It was the doctor who spoke.

Imogen opened her mouth to tell them there'd been a mistake. Why did they all think she was Isadora?

'She's been most stubborn, insisting on staying. Given her age and her frail health, I think we'll have her in, let her see for herself that you're all right, and then she can go home and get some rest. If you're feeling up to it, that is?' the doctor added.

Imogen sighed. Everything was happening too fast. She couldn't cope. She was feeling so shaky. So weak and vulnerable and guilty! She needed time to sort things out. And why, oh why did they insist that she was Isadora?

'Huh,' she said at last, since they were all looking at her expectantly. This they took for consent, for the doctor moved back towards the door and stepped outside.

The younger nurse helped her to sit up and fluffed the pillows around her. 'Don't worry about your pretty bracelet,' she said brightly. 'It's in your locker, here, along with your clothes.'

Bracelet?

And then Imogen understood. Of course! She'd still been wearing Isadora's bracelet when the plane had crashed.

She leaned her head back against the pillow and gave a small sigh. At least that was one mystery solved. But a moment later her stomach lurched as she registered what this must mean for the real Isadora. Her heart ached.

The door opened and an old woman, leaning heavily on an ivory cane, walked in. She was taller than Imogen had been expecting, and her silver-white hair was swept back off her face in an elegant chignon. She was wearing a summery white suit and pearl stud earrings. She looked exactly like what she was: a rich, well-groomed, elegant old woman, who must once have been stunningly beautiful. Beside her, a man towered over her, and Imogen felt her heart leap in sudden alarm. Two men had been demanding information about a woman called Dacres. Was this one of them?

As they came closer, however, she noticed his hand on the old woman's arm and the way he glanced down at her with concern, and forced herself to stop over-reacting. He was obviously a relative of Elizabeth Van Harte. Nothing at all to do with Robbie, and her current troubles and problems.

'Here she is, Elizabeth. Safe and only a bit battered, just like I told you,' the ginger-haired doctor spoke indulgently.

This woman is well-liked, Imogen realised, and as she approached the bed, her big brown eyes full of sympathy and concern, Imogen knew why. Her own aunt Joyce had been just such a woman as this. Kind, generous. A woman that everyone instinctively loved.

Imogen smiled, and Isadora's aunt smiled right back, and somehow, Imogen felt instantly better. It was like stumbling across a ray of sunshine in a bitter darkness.

Elizabeth reached out a bony, gnarled hand and grasped hers. 'I'm so glad you're all right, my dear,' she said softly, and the kindness and humanity in the wavery voice sent huge tears flooding into Imogen's eyes.

She quickly reached out and brushed the fat salty tears away. How on earth was she going to tell this wonderful woman that her niece was dead after all? That Isadora with the big brown eyes, just like this woman's, was dead, along with all the others on that doomed plane? She opened her mouth.

'Now, you can't stay long, Elizabeth,' the ginger-haired doctor said, watching her anxiously. 'I've told you before, your heart can only stand so much.'

Elizabeth Van Harte turned to him with a fond, weary smile. 'Dearest Giles, don't I always listen to you?'

'No,' he said, his eyes twinkling. The tall man beside Elizabeth chuckled, and Imogen's eyes finally flew to his face.

Standing at her bedside, he seemed to tower over her. He must be over six feet by a few good inches, she hazarded nervously. His hair was the dark gold of near-brown, with corn-coloured highlights. Dark-chocolate eyes looked down at her thoughtfully. Watchfully. They seemed to be boring into her, picking out her weaknesses, making her feel breathless.

She didn't know it, but with her long black hair loose around her shoulders, contrasting startlingly against the simple white hospital gown she was wearing, Imogen created an instant impression.

She was stunning. And he wasn't at all sure that he liked the way he was feeling. Imogen quickly looked away. She seemed to be having trouble with her breathing.

Sensing her unease, the doctor stirred. 'We mustn't over-tire Isadora just now. And . . . er . . . I was wondering if a counsellor . . . ?' His voice trailed off delicately.

'Yes, a good idea,' Elizabeth said at once. 'I'll arrange for one. You must to talk to somebody about what happened, my dear,' she murmured to Imogen. 'It's for the best.'

Imogen felt a renewed rush of dismay. Psychiatrists were expensive, and no doubt Elizabeth was paying for this hospital room. And all because she thought Imogen was Isadora. She couldn't let it go on.

But she was also scared to tell her why. She glanced at the doctor, remembering how worried about Elizabeth he was. If she just blurted out the truth, might she not give the poor old woman a heart attack?

'Doctor, excuse me.' Everyone turned to look as a woman in a darker blue uniform, obviously a matron, popped her head around the door. 'Could you please have a word with these two gentlemen? They insist on—'

'What on earth?' The doctor took a pace forward as the door opened fully and two men crowded in. Imogen had a quick glimpse of dark blue suits and hard faces, each holding a similar grim look.

'You can't come in here!' the matron squeaked, scandalised.

'Indeed you can't,' Giles said firmly.

'We're looking for Imogen Dacres,' one of the men said stubbornly. 'Is this her?'

'No, it isn't. Haven't you heard the latest press release?' Giles snapped. 'There was only one survivor of flight 203, and her name's Isadora Van Harte.'

The tall man at her side stared at the other two long and hard, his eyes narrowing ominously. Imogen could sense his anger, and also something else. His power – a kind of personal magnetism that seemed to tune in to her nerve endings and send them shivering deliciously.

Again her breath caught in her throat. Reluctantly, she dragged her eyes from his profile and towards the door. Both men were staring at her. Instantly, Imogen was reminded of a pair of wolves on the hunt. Something dark and frightening touched her spine, hissing a warning.

Elizabeth glanced down at the girl in the bed, and saw how even the little colour she had left had suddenly fled her face. Such lovely blue eyes the child had. And so beautiful. And so obviously scared.

The doorway was eventually cleared as the matron, with a smile of triumph, saw off the intruders. Giles came slowly back. 'Sorry about that,' he murmured. 'After a tragedy like this, I'd like to think they were genuine, but the fact is, they were probably reporters after a story.'

But Imogen knew beyond any doubt that they had not been reporters. And in that instant, she was utterly and totally certain: Robbie had been murdered. And somebody on this island knew all about it. Why else would those two goons be so anxious to find her? To track down Imogen Dacres?

So Robbie had been right to be afraid of his boss. This Morgan Dax.

Imogen was aware of fear again, but not the sudden, overwhelming fear that she'd felt on the plane. No. This was a colder, more creeping kind of fear.

For if someone could kill Robbie, they could kill her. Once they knew she was alive . . .

'You rest, my dear, you look exhausted,' Elizabeth said, once more squeezing her hand. 'And don't you worry about anything,' she added softly, her kindly brown eyes meeting Imogen's. 'You'll be all right.'

And as Imogen looked up at her, she suddenly understood what she had to do. What she had no other choice but to do.

'Thank you,' she said, her voice losing some of its croakiness now. 'Thank you, Aunt Elizabeth,' she added firmly.

THREE

The Grotto Bay Beach Hotel and Tennis Club was one of Bermuda's many top resort hotels, and, situated in Hamilton Parish, a popular spot with tourists and locals alike.

On a café terrace facing the sea, with its fine view of the power boats chopping white swathes through the blue ocean, Ellis Reynolds lifted a tall glass of clear water to his mouth and sipped appreciatively. The mandatory slice of lime floating on the top really had been freshly picked that morning.

It was barely 10 a.m. but already the day was warm enough for him to have discarded his white T-shirt, and the tan he was rapidly acquiring contrasted very attractively with his silvery-gold hair. Waitresses gave him the eye as they passed through the tables, carrying trays of drinks which sported tiny coloured umbrellas, sticks of celery and enough fruit to eat as a dessert. This was, after all, Bermuda.

Ellis smiled lazily at a dark-haired beauty sitting at a table near the terrace. She said something to her friend, who turned to look at him and then slowly lifted the sunglasses from her eyes to rest on top of her head. It was a definite invitation, and under other circumstances he would have taken them up on it. Why not?

He was thirty-two, single, an inch under six feet, lean and fit, and had eyes as green as a cat's, set in a sharply interesting face. Not surprisingly, therefore, that he'd been taken in hand by a variety of women. On the big, sprawling, vandal-packed estate in the East End of London where he'd grown up poor and hungry, there had always been women willing to teach Ellis Reynolds all there was to know about physical love. And Ellis, driven by a burning ambition to escape the estate and create a different life for himself, had always been grateful for what they'd taught him.

So now he gave a 'thanks but no thanks' smile, full of charming regret, and let his eyes sweep restlessly across the terrace instead. He'd been here two mornings already, having learned from a friendly bellhop that Averil Dax visited the café fairly regularly.

Ellis was beginning to wonder what the grinning bellboy had considered 'regularly'. Not that he minded waiting. The sea breezes were cooling and water-skiers, jet-skiers and parasailers were bright and distracting. The drinks were good and the huge tubs of colourful exotic flowers that littered the terrace were hardly an eyesore.

And he was patient.

Ellis had more in common with cats than just the colour of his eyes. He could wait at any particular mousehole for days and days if he had to. But today he didn't have to.

His deceptively lazy-looking, heavy-lidded eyes widened a fraction as he saw a woman step onto the terrace and look around for a free table. As luck would have it, there was one just to the right of Ellis, and she made her way slowly towards it. She wasn't tall, about five feet five or so, and had a dark-gold cap of hair swinging to points just under her chin. Big brown eyes in a heart-shaped face ensured that she was pretty rather than beautiful, but Ellis knew instantly who she was.

Averil Dax. Sister of Morgan Dax, one of the island's richest men, who ran a tourist-based business second to none. The name Dax, of course, had been shortened by a wily ancestor from Yugoslavia who, upon his arrival in New

York at the end of the last century, had quickly realised that nobody in his new adoptive land could pronounce his real name. From such wily beginnings, the Dax banking empire had been established within two generations.

Not that it was her brother or her family that Ellis was interested in.

He'd seen a picture of Averil Dax in the local paper, where she'd been shown attending the latest charity function. Ellis had found the sycophantic style of the columnist nauseating, but the picture of Averil Dax, caught as she stepped out of a limousine, was something he'd found highly interesting indeed. And not just because the short white cocktail dress she'd been wearing had suited her deeply tanned limbs to perfection, but because he'd recognised the man accompanying her.

Tony Jackson.

Ellis turned his head slightly away as Averil Dax approached, gazing fixedly out to sea. With his bare, muscled chest, tousled hair, sharp cheekbones and jaw, it was just as well he did, for Averil Dax gave him a quick double-take as she passed.

Ellis Reynolds was the kind of man any woman would pick out in a crowd.

She was not a native Bermudan, of course – both she and her brother had been raised in Boston. But when Morgan had moved to Bermuda, she had come to stay for a vacation, and had simply never left. Now, over five years later, she was used to seeing the influx of tourists come and go. And the golden-haired Adonis sitting at the table next to her looked like a typical tourist of the more wealthy kind.

Amused to find herself staring at him, she turned her chair slightly to one side, forced herself to study the menu and opted for the melon and passion fruit platter. She hadn't had breakfast yet, and could safely skip lunch if she gorged herself on fruit now. A waitress came and Averil gave her order.

She was wearing an old-gold coloured sheath which was square-necked and sleeveless, and was so simple in cut and style that anyone who knew anything about fashion would have instantly known that it was ruinously expensive.

Averil slowly leaned back in her chair and turned her face up to the sun. Only five minutes, she promised herself, then she'd put up the big sunshade that stood in the centre of the table. It was so easy to overdo the sun in Bermuda, something that she'd quickly learned from painful experience. Not that it ever seemed to worry Morgan. He never tanned to much beyond a wonderful golden nut colour no matter how often or how long he was out in the sun. And nowadays he spent more time diving than working in the office! Not that she could blame him for that, she mused, turning to look out at the deep blue Atlantic.

Many tourists were confused about the Atlantic, thinking it must be the Caribbean Sea. But Bermuda, as she was tired of pointing out to people, was not actually in the Caribbean! As she turned towards her brother's own private playground – the ocean – she found her gaze skidding to a halt, trapped by twin chips of emerald green.

Averil blinked.

The Adonis glanced casually away, giving her yet another glimpse of his sharp-faced, annoyingly attractive profile. Averil felt a shudder of attraction snake down her spine, and she sighed regretfully. He was obviously not interested. Besides, she wasn't really looking for a man in her life anyway, was she? Not after that near-fiasco with Roddy.

Roddy Cortington had been a friend since childhood, the only son of a steel magnate who'd long since agreed with her own parents that a marriage between Cortington Steel and Dax Investments would be ideal. Roddy hadn't minded the arrangement either. The only problem was, no one had told Averil. Friendship with the harassed and likeable Roddy was one thing, but marriage? Forget it! She was furious when she found out what was being planned for her, and unsurprisingly, neither her own family nor the Cortingtons had taken this very well. Such was the pressure they put on her she'd felt she simply had to get away from Boston and lie low for a while.

Naturally, she'd turned to Morgan, who promptly invited her to Bermuda. They'd always been close, and Morgan had always lived up to the role of protective older brother.

Her food came, and Averil smiled her thanks, sat up straighter and reached for her fork.

At his table, Ellis Reynolds watched her surreptitiously. He had to admit, that heart-shaped face of hers was very appealing. And she had that dainty way of moving some women had, which left him hard put not to stare at her. But then all desire to flirt promptly fizzled out and died as a dark-haired man stepped out onto the terrace and looked around. He was Italian in appearance, with black, slightly curling hair, a square, tanned face, and no doubt dark, snapping eyes which were concealed now behind expensive gold-framed sunglasses.

Averil noticed him at the same moment Ellis did, and he was amused and interested to note the way her face altered fractionally, as if she were just a little bit annoyed.

Tony Jackson smiled at her and walked forward confidently. With a small sigh, half annoyance, half resignation, she put down her fork and leaned back. 'Hi,' she said blandly, her American accent already becoming softened by the more drawling Bermudan influence. 'I didn't know you'd be here today or I'd have waited to order.'

'I was bored,' he said, flopping down elegantly into the chair beside her.

Ellis felt himself stiffening in instant and utter dislike, and told himself not to be such a fool. If he couldn't control himself better than this, just at his first sighting of his quarry, then he might as well pack up his bags and return to Amsterdam. He turned back to the sea, but his ears were tuned acutely to the conversation on his right.

'You're always bored,' Averil said teasingly, waiting politely as he ordered the same as her from the beaming waitress. Tony was famous for his lavish tipping.

'Too true. But you, *cara mia*, are always a cure for that particular malady.'

Ellis's lips twisted. Smooth as silk. Or grease! Averil, he would have been surprised to know, was thinking much the same thing.

Tony Jackson was a typical Bermudan resident – he was only there for half the year, had businesses worldwide, lived a playboy lifestyle that was all style and no life, and was good for a dinner and a dance and a few hours of pleasant flirting company. But that was all. Averil thought he'd understood that, but lately she was becoming worried that he might be reading more into their occasional dates than was good for him. Or her.

She really would have to make sure he understood. Her thoughts were distracted by the sudden wolfish and unmistakably sneering smile that crossed the face of her blond Adonis. Her eyes slewed to him, then quickly away again.

'Are you going to the Van Harte party this weekend? You're a big favourite of the old girl's, aren't you?' Tony asked lazily.

'Elizabeth? Yes to both. She's a sweetheart – a sort of stand-in grandmother.'

'I've been invited,' Tony said matter-of-factly. 'It's to celebrate her niece's arrival, isn't it? And the fact that she even survived to make it here, I shouldn't wonder.'

Like everyone else, he'd heard about the plane crash, caused, apparently, by a rare double strike of lightning that disabled the plane's electronics. When he'd heard about it, he couldn't help but laugh. Even outrageous luck was on his side, saving him the trouble of having to dispose of the annoying Imogen Dacres himself.

'You've been invited? You surprise me,' Averil drawled, her twinkling eyes telling him instantly that she was teasing him. He was, of course, invited to all the islands' big society bashes, as Averil well knew.

He lived in a beachfront mansion in Southampton, and as a single man was much in demand with all the matrons and mamas of the islands. It amused him to think how horrified they would be if they only knew that he was not the son of a count in Rome, as he told everyone, but the bastard of a Naples whore who'd tossed him out on his ear when he was fourteen because he wanted to kill her pimp and take his business.

Now he smiled charmingly and reached over to lay his hand across Averil's own. 'Want to come as my date?'

Averil smiled and slowly but firmly slid her hand out from under his, unknowingly making Ellis Reynolds' day as he covertly watched this manoeuvre. 'Sorry, Tony, I've already got a date.' She smiled as he scowled. 'Morgan.'

Tony shrugged. 'Ah. Morgan.' Sometimes having her big brother watching over her so closely annoyed Tony. But only a little In some ways he was rather pleased that Averil Dax had a chaperone and male presence like Morgan Dax in her life. After all, a man wanted the woman he'd decided to marry to be a lady. Not that he'd told Averil about his plans yet. He sensed she was still not firmly enough under the Jackson influence to be sure of her just yet.

He told everyone who asked him about his Anglo-Saxon name that he preferred to use the pseudonym rather than trade on his family's older, respected name, because he was determined to be his own man. His fictional older brother, Dino, was in line for the title, and it was the done thing for many second sons to strike out on their own.

Most people believed it because Tony Jackson was so obviously rich. So totally charming. So accomplished. He liked the opera. He was good-looking, and at forty-one, ripe for marriage. In reality, Jackson was the latest in a long line of aliases, necessary for him to keep one step ahead of the law.

'So, I suppose I shall have to go with that awful Mrs Coleman's daughter, Maisy,' he sighed woefully.

'Daisy,' Averil corrected him. 'And she's a very nice girl.'

Tony grunted, but with twinkling eyes, and began to eat. He was satisfied with his morning's work. And he would steal quite a few dances with Averil at the party.

Morgan Dax had nothing against him, although he suspected the entrepreneur didn't like him much; but Tony, after spotting Averil during his first week in Bermuda, had been careful to always keep on Morgan Dax's good side. A street fighter of the first order, Tony knew a dangerous man when he saw one. And Morgan Dax was one of the few men who could strike fear into Tony Jackson's dark and dirty heart. For although Tony had criminal contacts throughout the world, and had amassed for himself quite a large, if crooked fortune, Tony sensed that in Morgan Dax he had run across an even bigger tiger in the jungle.

Not that Dax was crooked. Or would know how to go about hiring a hit-man with just a phone call. But the man had brains. And money. And power. And, worst of all, courage. As a brother-in-law, he'd be a perfect smokescreen and an unwitting ally. As an enemy . . . well, Tony would just make sure that never happened.

He smiled a dazzlingly white smile at Averil, who didn't notice. She'd once again spotted a sardonic smile on the face of her Adonis, and was wondering why her heart was doing such strange flip-flops in her breast.

* * *

The next morning, Ellis was ready. He knew that Morgan Dax had a huge complex near Clarence Cove in the parish of Pembroke, a multi-level edifice set in acres of landscaped grounds which stretched all the way down to its own private beach.

He himself had rented the penthouse of a small but luxurious duplex near the Devonshire Dock, and had long since hired himself the use of an MG. As a boy, the small sports car had always represented the very essence of coolness and prestige.

He parked the car at the nearest public beach to Dax's place, stripped to a pair of dark green swimming trunks, put on his snorkel and entered the sea. It didn't take him long to reach the small area of private beach, and as he looked up the sloping rock face, past bushes frothing with the pink, red, yellow, white, blue, purple and orange flowers that Dax's Bermudan gardener seemed to prefer, he found himself whistling under his breath. Very nice.

Although he was wealthy himself now, and planned to be even wealthier by the time he was forty, he knew he was nowhere near to Morgan Dax's class yet. But give him time.

He trod water for nearly half an hour before he saw her. Dressed in a white one-piece swimsuit with a large straw hat on her head, she was walking down the recessed stone-and-wooden steps that had been cleverly cut into the cliff path, giving the residents access to the beach.

He waited until she'd spread out her towel and settled herself down with a book before lazily swimming into shore.

Averil, who loved classical English country-house whodunits, had just finished the chapter where the detective is invited to a gloomy mansion in Cornwall for Christmas, when she looked up and noticed a sleek pale head in the water.

She sighed. Even though there were huge signs at the beginning and end of the beach stating that it was private property, every now and then the odd tourist or two came ashore. She rose, not really angry, and walked to the water's edge, her book in one hand, the other shading her eyes in an effort to keep out the bright sun. She was not a snob any more than her brother, and they'd never yet got so paranoid about things that they'd prosecuted anyone for trespassing.

'Hi there!' she called out, watching the sleek head turn her way. 'This is private.'

The swimmer appeared to hear her, for he came closer, felt the beach beneath his feet, and rose. Averil squinted against the sun, wishing it wasn't directly in her eyes. All she could make out was a blur.

The man was walking towards her, and for just an instant, something in the animal way in which he moved, the easy-going power of his limbs, made Averil feel vulnerable.

She knew there were gardeners above her who'd come running if she screamed. And she herself was fit. Fit enough to run fast. She'd even taken a few self-defence lessons, at Morgan's insistence. Nevertheless, she took a step back as she noticed how well the swimmer filled the tight green trunks. The halo of sun around his head turned his fair hair intensely silver. And then his head blocked out the painful sunlight and she could lower her hand.

And found herself staring into twin emeralds again.

The Adonis!

Averil's lowering hand paused for a moment, and then continued on down to her side.

Ellis smiled. 'Hello. Did you say something?'

'Yes,' Averil said weakly. 'I said it was private property.' With the water plastering his hair to his scalp, Averil was even more aware than ever of the hard, uncompromising planes of his face. The hard line of his jaw. The strong, straight line of his nose. He was too intense-looking to be traditionally handsome, and yet she knew she'd never found a man more physically appealing.

'Oh, sorry,' Ellis said. 'When I heard you call, I thought you might want something.'

Averil found her throat becoming dry, and she almost laughed out loud. Want something? What could she possibly want from this magnificent creature?

Ellis was intrigued by the sudden flash of humour on her face and wondered what he'd said that was so funny.

'You're English,' Averil said at last.

'From good old London Town,' Ellis agreed. His cockney accent had been ironed out over the years, first by Oxford and then by Amsterdam. But it was still there. A perpetual reminder of his roots.

'Well, as I said, this is private property,' Averil repeated awkwardly. She was torn by a desire to get rid of him as quickly as possible, as her brain was dictating, and an equally strong desire to think of something to make him stay, as other, less reliable parts of herself were urging.

‘Oh. And am I going to get summonsed? Slung into jail? Will I have to kill scorpions with a sharpened plastic knife and tunnel my way out to freedom?’

Averil laughed. ‘Doubtful. I think I’ll let you off with a warning this time.’

Ellis grinned. ‘Well, that’s real kind of you.’

Something in his eyes, some hot glow which made them shine as no mere cold emerald could possibly shine, had the breath leaving her lungs in an unexpected whoosh. Her heart began to pick up the beat, like a bongo player suddenly finding another, faster, calypso rhythm. The smile slowly faded from her face. She could feel her nipples tightening beneath the demure white cotton, her knees weakening, and she blinked, taken aback.

She was not a virgin, of course. While attending Bryn Mawr, her college, she’d had a regular boyfriend, a zoology major, who’d left her at twenty-one to go to Alaska to study brown bears. After him there had been one other, a brief holiday affair here in Bermuda which had inevitably ended with him going back home to Melbourne. That experience had left her feeling slightly foolish – as if she’d made some kind of mistake when she was old enough to have known better.

Since then there had been no one. But she knew what her body wanted now. And she knew that this man knew. She even knew that it would be good. Very good. And why shouldn’t she take a lover? She was not promiscuous, by anyone’s standards. She always took precautions. She was a woman living in the twenty-first century and was well able to take care of her own body and emotional well-being.

So why was she this breathless?

And . . . let’s face it, a little bit scared?

It was Ellis, however, who made the first move. ‘Well, sorry again for interrupting your reading. I’ll let you get back to it.’ And with that he turned, giving her a glimpse of well-formed shoulders, and with a neat little tuck dive that showed off his tightly packed behind to perfect advantage, he was gone, leaving Averil chuckling to herself for no particular reason.

With a regretful sigh, she turned back to her book, but couldn't be bothered to read on and see who got murdered. Instead, her eyes followed the silver-gold head until it was out of sight – which wasn't long. He swam like he walked – with grace and power and economy of movement.

What a man. But obviously not a man who found her all that attractive. Averil sighed and tossed her book aside.

* * *

Cleaving through the water, Ellis Reynolds was cursing himself up one side and down the other. His body, pulsing as it was with sexual frustration, was more than happy to push itself to the limits in an attempt to burn off the unnecessary energy. What had made him turn tail and run like that? He hadn't been wrong in sensing that sudden, helpless, undeniable sexual attraction which had flared up between them. She hadn't wanted him to leave, he knew that.

But he'd also sensed a surprisingly touching reluctance in her though. A hint of vulnerability. Perhaps it had been that that had worried him. Or just good common sense?

Because she was mixed up with Tony Jackson. She was regularly seen on his arm. And that made Ellis wary. Very wary. Common sense and his own more finely tuned instincts told him that Averil knew nothing about Tony Jackson's true nature. As the sister of the mega-rich Morgan Dax, and a member of the highly respectable Dax banking family, it was almost impossible to believe that she knew how Tony earned his living.

And yet . . .

And yet it was too early in the game to show his hand. He had to be careful. Take it slow. Jackson was a dangerous enemy, and Ellis was not going to underestimate him.

Besides, he would see Averil again, he would make sure of that. He had to. She was his only passport to Tony

Jackson. And perhaps that was the true reason why he'd left her alone on the beach just now, with the nervous, puzzled fire in her eyes and the pounding of his own needs sizzling in his bloodstream.

Because he was using her.

And he didn't like it. He didn't like it one little bit.

Something told him she deserved more than that. Much more. And, even more worrying, he found himself wanting to give it to her.

FOUR

It turned out that Elizabeth lived so near the hospital, in a private residential area surrounded on nearly all four sides by the Bermuda Botanical Gardens, that Imogen could easily have walked to it. But, the following day, a dark American limousine was waiting outside the hospital entrance, and two nurses escorted her to it, despite her protests, in a wheelchair.

From inside, Elizabeth smiled up at her happily. 'Glad to be leaving?' she asked softly. Imogen sank into the car's cream leather upholstery with a sigh. All the bruises on her body seemed to be twinging in concert, like synchronised swimmers.

'Yes, I certainly am,' she agreed.

'Home, missus?' the chauffeur looked over his shoulder and gave both ladies a look of pure bonhomie.

'Yes please, Chance,' Elizabeth said.

The journey only took a few minutes, but Imogen craned her neck out the window, eager for her first glimpse of palms. The big green acreage of the botanical gardens themselves were magnificent. 'They look gorgeous,' Imogen breathed, real wonder in her voice.

'When you're feeling less stiff and sore, you must have a wander around,' Elizabeth said. 'They've got everything in there from woodlands to sub-tropical fruit gardens, and a frangipani collection you simply have to see. You'll love it.'

Imogen looked at her, feeling the twin stakes of guilt and remorse pierce her. But Elizabeth was looking better. There was a bit of colour to her sunken cheeks now, and a near-smile in her eyes. How could she jeopardise all that by blurting out that she was not her niece after all?

Besides, Imogen knew there was no going back, not now that it had gone so far. It would surely put her own life in danger.

For Imogen was now convinced that was the case. Somebody on this island – probably Morgan Dax, Robbie's one-time employer – was out to do her harm. Those goons, so anxious to trace her, had been a timely warning. She had no doubts at all that her life would be regarded as cheaply as Robbie's had. Whatever her brother had stumbled into, it was big, and it was dangerous. Fatally dangerous. But as long as everyone thought that Imogen Dacres was dead, she was safe. And as Isadora Van Harte, niece of the well-respected Elizabeth, she could nose around and ask questions, hopefully without too much difficulty.

Especially, her lips tightened grimly, about this Morgan Dax person.

Unaware of Elizabeth's eyes on her, watching the fleeting expressions of fear, pain and anger cross her face, Imogen leaned forward as the car drove into a quaint residential area of white walled, red roof-tiled bungalows, all with gardens frothing with bougainvillea and jasmine. It was so different from Kidlington! Back home it would be a dark and dismal November, complete with fog and rain. Here it was sunshine and flowers.

'Bermuda is wonderful,' she said softly. 'I've never been anywhere so lovely.'

Elizabeth nodded, just once, then, when Imogen turned to her, smiled. 'I'm glad you like it, Isadora,' she said softly. 'I hope you'll make your home here.'

Imogen flushed with guilt, for she knew that wasn't going to happen. As soon as she'd brought Robbie's killer to justice, she would have to return home. She couldn't afford to live in a place like this. 'Oh, Elizabeth,' Imogen said, trying to hide her misery behind a false smile. 'We'll have to see,' she added tremulously.

Once again, Elizabeth nodded to herself, and then took a deep breath. 'Well, here we are then. Home sweet home.'

Home sweet home turned out to be yet another sprawling whitewashed bungalow, but on a huge scale. As Imogen climbed stiffly out of the car, she could even hear a fountain tinkling away somewhere, and caught the gleam of a big blue swimming pool. As she stood on the paved driveway, staring up at the low, creeper-covered building, she felt as if she'd stepped into one of those magazines about the lifestyles of the rich and famous. Back at the hospital, when she'd smiled at Elizabeth and called her 'aunt', she'd been confused and scared and desperate to be safe. Now, realising what it would actually mean to play the part of a rich woman's niece, she wondered what on earth she'd been thinking of. She would never be able to pull it off.

'Come inside where it's cool. Grace, my housekeeper, makes a wonderful drink out of fresh limes and mangoes,' Elizabeth said, leading the way into her home, and, like someone being led to the gallows, Imogen followed.

* * *

She felt even worse the next day, when, having risen and breakfasted on fresh fruit and croissants, Elizabeth insisted that they go shopping.

'Nothing too strenuous, of course,' she smiled. 'I'm too old and you're still recuperating. But you need to get some clothes, and I know a lady who owns this pretty boutique in St George that you simply must see. She's amazing – she can take one look at you and know exactly what will suit you.'

Imogen could well believe that Elizabeth knew more about clothes than she probably ever would. The local chain stores had usually been her height of power-shopping!

'All right, but not too much, mind,' Imogen warned. She was determined to pay Elizabeth back every penny that she spent on her, and she was mindful that on her wages it might take her years if she let her 'aunt' go overboard!

'Oh pooh,' Elizabeth said. 'I want to indulge you – you've been through such a traumatic experience. Besides, I'm throwing a dance in your honour on Saturday, and you'll need something special for that.'

Imogen felt her breath whoosh out of her lungs and her eyes grew wide. 'A dance in my honour?' she repeated, stunned.

Elizabeth took in the pale, bruised face, the lovely dark blue eyes so full of surprise and awe, and felt her heart contract. Impulsively she reached out and grasped Imogen's hand in a tight grip. 'You deserve it,' she said softly.

But Imogen knew that she didn't. And she wondered, miserably, how she was ever going to live with her guilt for what she was doing now. Even though it was justified.

* * *

The boutique was on Duke of York Street, and the drive to St George's Island was a pleasure in itself. Chance deliberately slowed to a crawl when crossing 'The Causeway' which bridged the islands of Bermuda and St George. (There was a 20 mph speed limit which operated throughout the islands and was always rigorously enforced.)

At first it had seemed strange going at such a sedate pace. Back home, she was sure it would have driven the Oxford bus drivers insane! But she quickly became used to its advantages. Once, passing a small roadside bungalow, she actually had time to see tiny, jewel-like flashes around a bird feeder, and was told by Elizabeth that they were hummingbirds. Hummingbirds!

Imogen's face had glowed, her blue eyes softening in pleasure. Elizabeth told her that the bird feeders back home at Hartelands were located in the back gardens, and that any time she wanted to get a closer look at them, all she had to do was step outside and watch. Early morning, Elizabeth had added, was usually best.

Now they were in the town itself, pulling up outside the boutique, and it wasn't long before Imogen realised that Elizabeth hadn't exaggerated about her friend. The moment the two women stepped inside they were taken in hand by Bella, a warm Black woman with bright lipstick and impeccable taste.

'Bella, dear, this is Isadora. She needs a complete wardrobe,' was how Elizabeth introduced them.

Imogen paled. 'Oh, I wouldn't say that.'

She might just as well have saved her breath. Once Elizabeth was seated in a comfortable armchair and proffered drinks and cake by a shy assistant, Imogen became swamped with silken dresses of every colour imaginable. Chemises and T-shirts, blouses and jackets. Trousers and slacks and shorts and culottes. Scarves so floating and fine she could hardly feel them. Shoes, bags, belts. And, just as Elizabeth had predicted, everything she tried on fitted her to perfection.

Occasionally, when faced with a particularly lovely creation, Imogen stepped outside the changing cubicle to model it for Elizabeth, who watched her with gently smiling eyes and obvious contentment.

'We'll have them all,' Elizabeth said, watching the colour drain from Imogen's face and once again nodding at some private thought of her own.

'Excellent,' Bella said with alacrity, obviously pleased with the huge purchase order.

Imogen stared at Elizabeth in dismay, then went and crouched down beside her chair. 'Surely just one or two outfits is all I need,' she argued. 'A skirt and trousers and some mix-and-match tops. A couple of dresses, maybe, and just one evening outfit.'

'Don't be silly, Isadora,' Elizabeth said mildly. 'This is Bermuda. You'll be invited to many parties and social functions; do you really think you can wear the same outfit to all of them?'

Imogen's eyes flickered, and Elizabeth, sensing her discomfort, reached out and squeezed her arm. 'Please, let me do this for you. I want to. It's making me so happy. It's been so long since I've had anyone young and beautiful in my house. Or,' she leaned forward, her kind brown eyes shining with tears, 'or someone who needed me. Please, let me help you. Believe me, you've given me a new lease of life.'

Imogen bit her lip and sighed, knowing when she was beaten. 'Thank you, Elizabeth,' she said softly. And vowed silently to pay her back. Every penny. Somehow.

* * *

Over the next few days, Imogen took it easy and let herself heal. She did indeed watch the hummingbirds at the feeder, and then swam in the pool. Elizabeth insisted that Chance drive her around so that she could play tourist.

On her way to the Bermuda National Gallery at City Hall, or the spectacular Crystal Caves, or Fort Cunningham, she couldn't help but notice how many golf courses there were. They seemed to be everywhere, and Chance told her that there were more golf courses per square mile on Bermuda than in any other country.

She met most of Elizabeth's friends, who came to visit her at Hartelands, common sense telling her that she had to take things slow and easy, and firmly establish herself in her new identity. After all, it was the only protection she had.

Soon she would start to investigate Robbie's death properly. And then . . . She wouldn't have been human if the prospect didn't fill her with fear and dread.

* * *

The night of the Van Harte ball began with a magnificent sunset. All day long, caterers had been invading Grace's kitchen, and workmen had been busy stringing Chinese lanterns in the garden. A champagne fountain was painstakingly set up in the huge lobby, and the bungalow's terrace was cleared for action. Furniture in the library, main lounge and smaller rooms was pushed to the walls to make room for the guests.

Elizabeth confided to Imogen that she usually rented rooms in big hotels for her parties, but that she wanted this bash to be smaller and intimate and more 'homey'.

As Imogen watched chilled lobster and caviar being ferried in, and waiters in tuxedos setting up shop, she wondered what Elizabeth's idea of 'ritzy' must be!

With time pressing on, she went to her room. It was white, peach and pale green, with an en-suite bathroom in sea-green and gold. In there she ran water into the sunken tub.

Her first night in the four-poster bed, swathed with fine gauze curtains, had been a restless one, for she had felt like a fairytale princess. Even now, as she ran the tub and poured in a measure of gardenia-scented bath salts from Paris, she felt both torn with guilt and alive with excitement and happiness.

All those years of scrimping and saving and looking after her mother now seemed to be another world away. But, as she lowered herself into the warm, gloriously scented water, she firmly reminded herself that this world could only be temporary.

She washed her long dark hair and on stepping out of the bath wrapped a fleecy towel around them, slipping into a silk peignoir and walking to her vanity table to use the hairdryer. She was pleased to note that all but three of her bruises had faded completely, including those on her face. Once her waist-length raven locks were dry, she slipped on lacy white briefs and a bra which hooked in the front and lifted and thrust her breasts together.

Bella had been surprised by Imogen's lack of knowledge about sexy lingerie. Now, donning a pair of the sheerest of silk stockings, nervously careful not to put her finger through them, Imogen walked to her newly filled wardrobe and took a deep breath before opening it.

She went straight to the evening-wear section, feeling cold with nerves. She tried to fight back the panic, telling herself that Bella had given her only the best, and that no matter which dress she chose, it would be 'right'.

Yet she couldn't help but think that all the other women coming to this ball tonight would know all there was to know about what colour was in vogue, and what was *de rigueur* and what was not. They would have grown up with panache and social grace, as, no doubt, had the real Isadora Van Harte. Standing there in her new fancy underwear, facing the intimidating galaxy of clothes, Imogen suddenly felt very much like the humble secretary from Oxford.

Oh, stop it, she told herself angrily. You're here for Robbie, nothing else.

Her hands, wandering through the clothes hangers, hesitated on an ice-blue shimmering sheath. It was slender and elegant, and she vaguely remembered that it had a slit up one side to allow for easy walking. With her dark blue eyes and black hair, it had looked good in the shop. Hadn't Bella almost gasped when she'd put it on? That settles it, Imogen thought with a wry smile. Anything that could make Bella gasp was the gown for her! Before she could dither and change her mind, Imogen slipped the gown over her head and, with a little difficulty, zipped it up the back. She donned a pair of slingback kitten heels in a blue which almost perfectly matched her eyes. Walking to her mirror she checked her appearance.

The dress was perfect, with a glittering beaded fringe coming diagonally across her breasts, leaving one shoulder bare, the other arm encased to the wrist in clinging ice-blue silk. The slit up the leg seemed longer than she remembered, coming up to past her mid-thigh. Oh well.

Nervously Imogen sat in front of the mirror and rooted through her rather sparse make-up bag. Her pale face required a touch of blusher, and for her lips she chose a dark, mysterious shade of plum. Next, she applied a layer of lash-extending mascara that Bella had assured her would do wonders for her eyes. As it did.

Finished, Imogen found herself blinking in amazement at the creature in the mirror. With her newly washed hair like a curtain of black silk falling down her back, and her eyes the dark mysterious blue of a deep ocean, she almost failed to recognise herself.

Just then there was a tentative knock at the door. 'Come in.'

Elizabeth, looking resplendent in a gold gown and, yes, a diamond tiara in her grey mass of curls, took a few steps into the room and stopped dead, leaning on the inevitable cane. She stared at Imogen for so long that the girl felt herself beginning to panic. I've got it all wrong, Imogen thought. This dress isn't suitable. Or my hair. I knew I should have had it put up. Was it too girlish, too 'young' for her to wear it down?

'My dear,' Elizabeth said at last, her voice almost choked with emotion. 'You're the most beautiful thing I've ever seen.'

Imogen felt herself almost wilt. 'Oh, is that all?' she said, and then wondered why Elizabeth laughed so heartily.

'Wait right there, I have just the thing,' the old lady said mysteriously, and hurried out of the room.

Imogen dabbed some Poison by Dior behind her ears and on each wrist.

'Here, try these on,' Elizabeth's voice broke into her thoughts and Imogen looked up as her aunt walked towards her.

Imogen's eyes flickered. Her *aunt*! Since when had she started thinking of Elizabeth as her real aunt? The trouble was, it was so easy to do. Elizabeth was such a loving, kind, wonderful woman, Imogen felt as if she really was her aunt. Or did she merely wish that she was?

Elizabeth snapped open the flat blue case she was carrying – and Imogen gasped. Lying on a bed of cream silk was a spectacular sapphire and diamond necklace and matching drop earrings.

She backed away hastily. 'Elizabeth, no.'

'Nonsense – they'll go perfectly with that outfit. Now don't tell me you can't borrow my jewellery if I want you to.'

Imogen shook her head. The only time she'd seen jewels like these was when a student at St Bede's had received a catalogue from Asprey and had shown it to the admin staff.

She was shaking – literally shaking – as Elizabeth looped the necklace around her neck and fastened it, her old, gnarled hands gently lifting the swathe of hair out of the way. 'Now the earrings,' she insisted, and Imogen fiddled them on. Looking at herself in the mirror, the gems at her throat and ears sparkling in the light, she felt humbled.

'Thank you, Elizabeth,' she said chokingly. 'They're wonderful.'

Just then a car horn tooted outside. 'Ooh, our first guest,' Elizabeth said, the excitement in her voice catching. 'Come on. I hope it's Averil. I can tell the two of you will get on like a house on fire.'

Imogen let herself be led down into the lion's den.

It was nearly eleven before the last of the guests arrived, and by now the orchestra which was set up in the big lounge was playing 'Moon River', and guests both in the house and in the gardens were swaying intimately to the music. The champagne fountain looked set to flow until dawn, and waiters circulated from the kitchens with a never-ending stream of smoked salmon, crab, lobster and other melt-in-the-mouth delicacies.

Imogen was at last beginning to relax. The first guests had been a distinguished diplomat and his wife, and Imogen had nervously greeted them, sure that the word 'FRAUD' must have been written in big letters right across her forehead.

But as the house gradually filled, and Imogen slowly came to realise that these were not monsters, just people, she began to feel better. She was, however, very firm with married men who tried to flirt with her. Ever since her near-miss near-affair with Professor Francis Dwyer she was wary of men.

Imogen was just beginning to think that there really was nothing to this high society entertaining lark when she saw, stepping through the French windows and onto the terrace, the man who'd been with Elizabeth when she'd first come around at the hospital.

At the time, he hadn't said a word to her, for there'd been no real opportunity for them to talk. But the instant he stepped onto the terrace, Imogen was aware of him. His height. The way the dark-gold hair shone under the nearby red paper lantern. The lean grace of his figure in a white tux. Her whole body seemed to change gear.

Leaning against the stone balustrade, an unwanted glass of champagne in her hand, Imogen felt herself stiffen, like a cat sensing a dog coming into the room.

He smiled and spoke to someone, reached for a drink, looked casually around and found her. She didn't know it, but she stood spotlit under a white paper lantern, and he felt his breath stall. The beaded fringe of her dress shimmered, as did the jewels on her pale skin, making her look almost otherworldly.

Slowly he moved forward. Her long black hair slithered over the stone balustrade beside her, over her arm, one long tendril of it tumbling over her breast. He'd never seen hair that long, that thick, that midnight black before. And, as he got closer, those eyes! Dark as a mountain lake.

Imogen watched him approach, feeling trapped by the balustrade and not at all sorry. She smiled uncertainly. 'Hello. I'm glad you could come,' she said at once, feeling compelled to burst into speech. There was something about the way he was watching her that scared her.

And aroused her.

How very English, was his first thought. The voice was as cool as the rest of her. She looked so composed he wanted to ruffle her, just to see what lay beneath.

'I'm glad to be here,' he said sardonically. 'Dance?'

And before she could stop him, his arm came around her waist and they were moving. She didn't even get the chance to tell him that she didn't dance. That she'd never really learned how. He pulled her out onto lawn as soft as carpet, and smiled as her foot trod on his toe. Imogen blushed and quickly stepped off. She was painfully aware of the strength of his arm around her back. The warmth of his hand where it was splayed against her spine. The pine scent of his after-shave. He pulled her closer still. Again she stumbled onto his toe. Her breathing became agitated. 'I'm sorry, I'm not very good at this,' Imogen said numbly.

'At what?' he asked, his voice so insinuating that she blushed.

'At dancing!'

She could barely hear herself over the pounding of her heart. She'd heard about this, of course, this thunder-and-lightning moment of instant attraction. But she'd never thought it was really real. And had certainly never thought that it could happen to her.

'I'd never have guessed,' he half-laughed. 'Good job I'm wearing reinforced toecaps.'

'Liar,' she shot back and laughed. She couldn't help it. She was dancing under an island moon, wearing diamonds and sapphires, with a man who was sending her pulse rate skyrocketing. She would have been less than human if she didn't feel blissfully happy.

The orchestra segued seamlessly into the theme tune from *Dr Zhivago*, and she felt herself being pulled closer still. Her bent knee brushed against his leg, and all at once, her heart began to dance far better than her feet ever could.

She looked up into his face; the dark eyes, melting over her. She felt his own breathing stumble and smiled at herself. For a woman who'd never made love to a man in her life before, she was feeling supremely confident.

This man was hers. I'm . . . Imogen, she wanted to say. Imogen Dacres. But of course she couldn't, and her eyes clouded. She closed them for a second.

Oh, to start off with a lie. A lie for this man, of all men. It felt so wrong. So treacherously wrong.

But there was no help for it. She opened her eyes again and looked at him adoringly.

'I'm Isadora,' she said softly.

The stranger holding her in his arms smiled gently. 'I'm Morgan Dax,' he said.

FIVE

Imogen froze. She could feel the entire planet beneath her feet shift, making her stumble.

Morgan felt her push against him unsteadily and smiled. 'You really aren't very good at this, are you?' he murmured, a strange tenderness tickling him around the heart.

'No,' Imogen said faintly. 'I'm not.' And fought back the hysterical laughter which threatened to overwhelm her.

She'd come to the island to investigate Robbie's death, and what was the first thing she did? Almost fall head over heels for the man who was the prime suspect.

No, she was definitely not very good at this at all. She just had to face it: she was no damned good at picking men. If she thought Francis Dwyer had been a near catastrophe, he was nothing compared to this folly!

She'd been twenty-two when Francis Dwyer had first come to St Bede's, a junior research fellow in Oriental Studies. He was young and good-looking and was the instant darling of the admin office and quite a few female students. She had been flattered when he'd started paying her particular attention, and was thrilled to be invited to Browns for lunch. She'd been more than happy to go punting with him on the Cherwell, and was breathless with anticipation when he invited her to a quaint and lovely seventeenth-century Cotswold hotel for the weekend.

She'd been packing for that weekend, a little scared, a little elated at the thought of taking a lover for the first time, when a friend of hers from work had phoned to gossip.

And the bombshell fell. Had she heard about Professor Dwyer? He was married! Apparently his older but wealthier wife had stayed in Japan for a few months to sell their house before following her husband to Oxford.

Needless to say, Imogen never got to the lovely Cotswold inn. And never got to lose her virginity. It had been a short, sharp shock, and one she'd never really got over. Ever since, all of the men who pursued her had left her cold. Until this man. Until this moment. And now another short, sharp shock. It was so funny it was almost classic.

So funny she could cry!

She took a ragged breath and forced back her self-pity, making herself look up into his eyes again, prepared to face reality head on once more. It was over before it had ever really begun. Well, she could cope with that. She'd just bloody well have to. Her hardened blue eyes met his dark ones and she froze once more. He was looking at her in a very odd kind of way.

She guessed at once that she must have been advertising her feelings like a neon sign. She must look like a stricken nanny goat! Fool! Fool! She forced herself to smile. 'I never really learned to dance properly,' she managed to mumble. 'Sorry.'

Morgan continued to stare at her. What had upset her so? Something obviously had. One moment she was all sparkling eyes and confidence, the next . . . His eyes narrowed. And over her head his eyes sought out Elizabeth.

Elizabeth Van Harte had been his first real friend on the island, reminding him, as he supposed she must remind everyone, of his favourite aunt. Not surprisingly, over the years he'd come to look on her in just that capacity. If someone was trying to do her down . . .

He looked back down regretfully into the lovely face beneath his, noting the shuttered look, the tense shoulders and grimly held lips. The only reason he could think of for her sudden caution was the fact that his name had triggered her odd response. And the only reason for that must be her realisation that she was now dancing with someone who was likely to be in Elizabeth's corner. For everyone knew that both he and Averil looked on Elizabeth as family.

He felt himself slowly tensing up, and as the dance drew to an end was glad to step away from her. With his body yearning to stay close while his mind was screaming at him to take a step back, he wasn't enjoying the tug-of-war much. Nevertheless, he took her elbow in a firm grip as she tried to pull away and led her back to the terrace, to a quiet table in a corner under some pale lilac clematis. He brushed a tendril of dark hair aside and watched it fall back on her shoulder. Hell, she was lovely.

'How are you and Elizabeth getting along?' he asked smoothly, shrugging out of his jacket and leaving it draped over the back of the chair.

Imogen licked her lips, which felt suddenly dry. 'Fine. More than fine. She's dear.'

Morgan, in the act of taking off his black bow tie, hesitated, wondering over her choice of words, then realising how easily she'd found exactly the right one. Elizabeth was dear.

'I'm glad you think so,' he said softly.

At the sound of unmistakable warning in his voice, Imogen's head shot up. She met his bland, dark eyes and felt herself flush guiltily. Again, all her misgivings about deceiving the old lady washed over her.

Morgan watched her face like a hawk scanning a field for voles. 'I'd hate to think anyone was trying to take advantage of her,' he pressed relentlessly. And from the way she shifted nervously in her chair, knew he had scored a hit.

He felt a surprisingly painful punch of disappointment hit him, low down in the abdomen. He knew only a little about the Van Harte family history. That Elizabeth, who'd never married, had inherited most of her family's money because her only brother had had some kind of a row with their parents. He'd been either cut off without a penny, or sent into exile, or something equally final, and Elizabeth, as far as he knew, had had no contact thereafter, only learning of her brother's death after his funeral had already taken place. And had obviously always bitterly regretted it. He remembered her face, shining with excitement when she'd told him last month that her niece was coming for a visit at last. What a damned pity it was that the niece was only looking out for number one. How else to explain the guilt that was obviously eating at her? Did she think she was going to fleece Elizabeth of her money? Or was she aiming to worm her way into her aunt's will? Either way, she'd have to be watched.

Morgan sighed and beckoned a passing waiter. 'Champagne?' he asked smoothly.

Thoughtlessly, Imogen shook her head. 'No thanks. I don't drink much.'

Morgan's eyes narrowed. Very cleverly done. He almost believed her. 'My my. You can't dance, you don't drink. Hardly a typical Van Harte, are you?' he taunted, taking a sip of the drink as the waiter melted discreetly away.

Imogen tensed. Damn, damn, damn. She was going to have to be more careful! She was sure the real Isadora knew how to party properly! 'I used to drink a bit too much,' she lied valiantly. 'So now I'm extra careful.'

It sounded reasonable, he thought. Just the sort of thing that could easily happen to a girl who'd always had life too easy. But, for some reason, Morgan didn't believe her. 'You're lying to me,' he said flatly, and watched her nearly jump out of her skin. Her wide, fathomless blue eyes fixed on him like a rabbit being hypnotised by a snake.

Morgan felt his heartbeat refusing to be tamed. Something primitive and primordial, something he hadn't felt around a woman before, kicked itself into being. It scared him. And that made him angry. Morgan Dax wasn't used to being scared.

Slowly he leaned across the table. 'Be very careful, little girl,' he said softly. 'I'm not a man who can be played with.'

Imogen already knew that. Oh yes, she already knew that.

But it wasn't going to put her off. She was not Robbie; unprepared, easy-going Robbie. She was here for justice. And if it meant taking on this man, then that was just what she was going to do. After all, what did she have to lose? With her mother and brother dead there was nobody left in the world who would miss her if she miscalculated. And although she was scared, she was not scared to the point of defeat.

She blinked, amazed by her self-discovery. She was strong!

'I think you'll find, Mr Dax,' she said just as softly, leaning across the table herself and smiling coolly, 'that I'm not much for playing games, either.'

Morgan felt himself begin to smile, and ruthlessly cut it off before it could reach his lips. The arrogant, saucy little . . . Was she actually daring him . . . Slowly he leaned back, rapidly reassessing the situation.

'So you like a challenge?' he asked thoughtfully, his eyes narrowing as he cocked his head slightly to one side as he regarded her. She was certainly different. A contrast of opposites. Shy and yet a would-be recovering alcoholic. A novice on the dance floor, yet confident enough to take him on, head to head.

A clematis petal fell and landed on her raven tresses, and he caught his breath. He was going to have to be careful. Very careful. But then, he smiled wolfishly, so was she.

'Challenges don't interest me,' Imogen said dismissively, getting to her feet, needing to get out of there and wishing her legs didn't feel so weak. She was suddenly dog-tired. 'Only results.' And with that exit line, she turned and left him.

Puzzled.

There was something going on here, Morgan knew it. Something, perhaps, more complicated than an ostracised niece wanting to get back into line for her cut of the family fortune. He hadn't carved out his own multimillion-dollar business empire, independent of his family, without honing his hunter's instincts to a fine point. The annoyingly beautiful, tantalizing Isadora Van Harte was up to something. And Morgan was going to make it his business to find out what.

He caught Elizabeth looking over at him, a gently smiling, speculative look on her face, and he raised his glass in a salute to her. Elizabeth smiled and saluted back, then glanced away, watching the beautiful girl in ice-blue weave her way through the party. Her own eyes were thoughtful. It was high time, she thought approvingly, that Morgan Dax was given a run for his money. And unless she was wrong (and Elizabeth seldom was) the beautiful stranger from England was just the girl to give it to him!

* * *

Tony Jackson was dancing the final waltz, not with Averil Dax as he'd hoped, but with an anonymous younger daughter of a father who ran an aircraft supplies business on St David's. It was nearly three before he finally got away from her and into his scarlet Maserati. He was not in the best of moods.

Although he'd managed quite a few dances with Averil, he knew he was not making the kind of progress with her that he wanted to. She'd spent most of her time talking to the old relic who was throwing the bash and fending off the other young bucks. Still, at least she was fending them off, he thought with a self-satisfied smile.

He drove to his beach house, parked haphazardly, and let himself in. Detouring en route to his bedroom, he poured himself a double Scotch and checked his fax. A regular 'client' of his had an 'item' he'd like to buy. From the fictional name of his client, he knew that the item would be a work of art.

One of Tony's main sources of income came from arranging for the theft of specific works of art from private collections to be sold on to his client. It was understood, of course, that the new collector could never show his latest acquisition in public.

Tony shrugged and took his drink to his bed – a large, circular revolving affair that would have had Averil in stitches, had he but known it. For all his flair, Tony's taste wasn't the best.

He finished his drink and, restless, rose and went to the big picture window. The moon was full and high, but he barely registered its beauty as it silvered the calm waves.

So that had been Isadora Van Harte, he mused, picturing again the woman at the ball. A real and rare beauty, and no mistake. But Tony hadn't been seriously tempted. He too knew that she was the 'poor' relation of the Van Hartes, and might never come into any of the sizeable Van Harte fortune. Although the old crone, Elizabeth, seemed happy enough with her. But no, he'd stick with Averil.

Down below, the waves lapped at the sandy beach, and he gave a cruel, satisfied smile as he thought of the unknown Imogen Dacres, now dead at the bottom of the ocean. Hers had been one of the few bodies they'd never recovered.

The accident investigation team had retrieved enough of the wreckage of the plane to pronounce the accident due to a freak lightning strike, and soon, he knew, the tragedy would be forgotten. No one wanted to be reminded of death when they already lived in an earthly paradise. Besides, it was bad for the tourist business.

With a snort of laughter, he turned from the window and began undressing. Besides, it served the bitch right. And it was ironic she died the same way as that no-good, two-timing bastard of a brother of hers. In the ocean. He cursed all the Dacres as he slipped between the black satin sheets. It was because of them he'd lost a fortune.

He knew he should stop thinking about it now, that it would only work him up into a fury if he didn't, but he couldn't stop himself. When he thought of those missing diamonds . . . He cursed, sitting up and dialling the number of a madam he knew. He desperately needed a woman tonight. Any woman.

He roundly cursed Averil Dax while he was at it.

* * *

Ellis watched the parascending boats for a long time before suddenly sitting bolt upright. He was sitting at a café overlooking Hamilton Harbour, halfway between the ferry terminal and the impressive Princess Hotel, doing nothing more than passing the time of day, when he saw her.

Averil Dax.

She was walking along the beachfront dressed in a big straw hat, sunglasses and a long, floating white dress which reminded him of gothic horror stories, where the maiden was about to get it in the neck from Christopher Lee. Before he knew it, he too was on his feet, following her onto a pier bearing the logo 'Dax Parascending'.

He knew her brother had his fingers in all areas of water sports, and as he watched, two racy-looking boats in red and green moved away from the pier, each containing an excited-looking man and woman. A honeymoon couple, he wondered idly. He knew Bermuda did a roaring trade in that area.

As he watched, a few minutes later two canopies slowly rose from behind the boats, their cheerful colours dotting the vast blue sky. The couple waved at each other frantically. He could almost imagine he could hear their shrieks and laughter.

Now that looks like fun, Ellis thought. He was standing there, still watching, when he suddenly became aware of a presence beside him and quickly looked around. His green eyes glowed. 'Hello,' he said amiably, and without the least trace of surprise. 'Is that recommended after a full breakfast?' he asked, and nodded towards the speeding boats and high, floating canopies.

Averil laughed. 'Not if you're faint-hearted as well,' she warned.

'Never let it be said,' Ellis grinned. 'I was thinking of giving it a go. Want to come and hold my hand?'

'Only if I had arms fifty feet long.'

Ellis checked out her long, slender limbs and raised an eyebrow. Averil felt herself shiver. Nicely.

'How about coming along just to shout encouragement then?' he murmured. 'For someone who's never had his feet off the ground in his life.'

Averil slowly took off her sunglasses and looked him in the eye. 'All right,' she said softly. 'I'd hate to see you tied to the ground.'

Ellis grinned. Hell, she was quick!

'Deal,' he said, and reached out his hand. Solemnly she took it.

'We'll have to wait our turn,' she told him, turning back and leading him onto the pier where several others were waiting ahead of them. 'But it won't be long. As soon as Barry sees there are more customers waiting he'll ring through for more boats.'

'Your brother seems to have it all organised,' Ellis said admiringly, and Averil shot him a quick glance. He was wearing dark blue shorts which revealed strong columns of lightly haired golden legs, and a polo shirt of pale aqua that ruffled around his arms and midriff in the sea breeze. The glare of the sun made the corners of his eyes crinkle attractively. She'd noticed him the moment she'd leaned against the rails to watch the boats. Her inner radar had already been tingling an excited warning before she'd even glanced up.

Never one to look a gift horse in the mouth, she'd gone to him at once. Now she wondered if this meeting was as coincidental as she'd previously thought. Although she was willing to admit to the possibility that it was a benign karma bringing them together all the time, she was well aware that there were other, more worldly explanations.

'You know my brother?' she asked, oh so casually.

Ellis turned to her, not mistaking the caution in her voice. 'I know of him,' he corrected gently.

Averil turned and leaned against the railing, trying to pretend the answer to this next question wasn't as vitally important as it really was. 'And are you expecting to do business with him?'

Ellis noted the downward look of her lovely brown eyes, the tense quiver of her lips, and felt his heart melt. 'Since I'm in import and export I don't see how we could have any business in common, do you? I'm here strictly for a vacation,' he lied, then added truthfully, 'I haven't had one in over five years.'

And he wondered, with a pang of sympathy, how often men used her to try and get an introduction to her brother. From the shiny-eyed look of relief she gave him, probably quite a few times, he guessed grimly. 'I only know about him because I asked around about you,' he added softly.

Averil felt her mouth go dry. So he *had* been interested that day at the café. And on the beach.

'Oh,' she said softly. Then blinked. 'It's our turn.'

Ellis helped her onto the boat, fighting back an absurd twinge of jealousy when she smiled at the driver and his helper, calling them both by name. They headed out to sea at a fair clip, the noise of the engine, the wind in their hair and the cry of the gulls overhead drowning out any attempt at speech. Not that Ellis minded. It was enough just to look at her. And know.

And they did look at each other. Long, unsmiling, but strangely easy looks.

He admired this woman. She didn't regard herself cheaply, hence the subtle interrogation about her brother. And she wasn't on the hunt, as she'd made clear with her none-too-subtle reference about tying him to the ground.

Although he wouldn't mind being tied down by Averil Dax, he thought suddenly. In fact . . .

Before he could get thoroughly rattled by the continuation of that thought and where it would inevitably lead, the boat slowed down. The one called Russell turned to Ellis, a contraption of belts and ropes in his hand.

'Right. Have you parascended before?'

'No. I haven't.'

Averil grinned as Ellis donned the harness and Russell buckled him in. He listened carefully to the instructions he was given, and Averil found herself wishing she was going up there with him. To float above the sea with this man would be heaven indeed.

Ellis turned and caught her gaze. Slowly, he smiled. There was something knowing in his look that riled her, and yet it was mixed with something both gentle and vulnerable, which soothed her. Slowly he raised an eyebrow. 'Wish me luck?'

'You won't need it,' she said certainly. He was the kind of man, she knew, who could cope with anything. She leaned backwards with the impetus as the boat shot forward and gathered speed, and watched with a thudding heart as he was slowly and smoothly lifted into the air.

Ellis felt his feet leave the warm decking of the boat with a jolt that wasn't quite fear, nor quite excitement. Then, as the harness held and he began to feel safe, he felt the thrill of freedom. He watched the uncoiling of the rope on the deck as he went up and back.

Averil watched him moving away from her and felt absurdly bereft. It was ridiculous, she knew. She'd barely spoken a few words to him. Had only seen him three times before. She didn't even know his name! And yet . . .

Ellis kept his gaze on her until she was no more than a white and gold pattern on the deck, and then he was flying high and looking down at the white trail from the boat. He looked slowly around, at the turquoise of the sea, the paler blue of the sky. A fellow parascender, going the other way, waved. He waved back. But as exhilarating as the experience was, both new and interesting, he wanted to get back to the boat. Because Averil Dax was there, waiting for him. Waiting for him to make love to her.

As they both knew he would.

But what then, Ellis? he asked himself. As he looked down on her from his great height, he could see in his mind's eye her liquid chocolate eyes, her heart-shaped face, her trusting, tender mouth. What will you do then?

Ask her about Tony Jackson? Angle an invitation onto that fancy yacht of his? Become just another man in a long line, using her to get something you want?

Ellis swore graphically, and for the first time ever, wished he'd never come to Bermuda.

SIX

Imogen walked into the hospital foyer with the box of Belgian chocolates clasped loosely in one hand. Asking for Caroline and Gerta, the nurses who'd looked after her, she was directed to a long ward bedecked with flowers and bowls of fruit.

Gerta, the older one, spotted her first and gave a small squeak of surprise and welcome. 'Miss Van Harte! Hello! Oh, you're looking so much better. All the bruises are gone now.'

Imogen smiled warmly. 'I just wanted to come in and thank you all for looking after me,' she said, holding out the beribboned box of expensive chocolates.

Gerta's eyes lit up. 'Bless you. I'll put these in the staff room fridge. But we'd better not let Matron see them!'

Imogen grinned. 'How is Matron?'

'Sitting in on the monthly board meeting. Plebs versus the Titans, we call it.'

Imogen laughed. 'Well, I won't keep you. I just wanted to meet you again under more normal circumstances, minus the gatecrashing reporters,' she added craftily.

Gerta sighed. 'Between you and me, those two were no more reporters than my aunt Fanny's Pekinese.'

Imogen felt a cold snake slither down her spine. 'You know, I thought that at the time,' she said, allowing a slightly puzzled frown to tug at her brows. 'But what with the headache and the drugs I'd been given, I thought I was probably reading too much into it. To tell the truth,' she said, confidentially lowering her tone and standing a step nearer, 'they rather scared me. I was glad I wasn't that woman they were looking for.'

Gerta, impressed to be in the confidence of the rich and beautiful Isadora Van Harte, nodded solemnly. 'I know what you mean. I heard on the grapevine that those two had been at the hospital ever since the news got out that there was a survivor from the plane crash being brought in.'

Imogen didn't have to pretend to shudder. 'Spooky. Did you recognise them at all?' she asked, trying not to hold her breath.

But disappointingly Gerta shook her head. 'No. Mind you, one of the girls who serves in the canteen said she was sure that they worked for one of the rich playboy types on the island, as a sort of bodyguard team. But that can't be right, can it?'

Imogen forced herself to smile. 'Hardly. Unless one of the island bigwigs needs protecting from a mere woman.' And she laughed, grimly. So, they were hired muscle were they? Not surprising, but nice to have it confirmed, she supposed. Now all she had to do was trace them to Morgan Dax, or whoever.

She knew she didn't want it to be Morgan Dax, and was annoyed at herself for being so feeble. Just because she'd felt so complete and content, dancing in his arms that night. Nevertheless, she wasn't about to go accusing anybody of anything until she had proof. That was only fair.

But, oh, don't let it be Morgan!

'Uh-oh, here's Matron,' Gerta suddenly said. 'The meeting must be over.'

'I'll just nip off then,' Imogen said hastily, and added softly, 'I hope you enjoy the chocolates.'

She left via the hospital's main entrance, unaware that Morgan Dax, in the process of opening the door to his gold

Jaguar XJS, spotted her the moment she stepped into the sunlight.

She was wearing a summer dress of pale blue scattered with bright scarlet poppies and white daisies, with gauzy sleeves which covered her arms. She looked spectacular, but Morgan noticed that she was frowning as she emerged from the entrance.

Both he and Elizabeth, as island dignitaries with big pockets, were governors, and regularly attended the hospital board meetings. Now he watched her cross the car park, puzzled to note that instead of turning towards the residential district where Elizabeth had her home, she turned instead towards the bus stop at the bottom of South Road.

Since he knew that Elizabeth had insisted she go everywhere in the car, with Chance to drive her, he was instantly suspicious. Just where was she going that she didn't want anybody to know about? For the fact that she must be up to something was, to Morgan at least, fairly self-evident. Why would any self-respecting gold-digger travel by humble bus, when she had a chauffeured limousine at her beck and call?

Quickly, he climbed into his car and turned on the engine, pulling up several yards behind the bus stop. And sure enough, a few minutes later, she joined the queue.

Morgan caught his reflection in the mirror and smiled wryly at himself. He was getting obsessed with the lovely, scheming Isadora Van Harte and he knew it. The trouble was, he couldn't stop himself. Didn't *want* to stop himself. He'd never felt this alive since deciding to leave the safety of the family business and strike out on his own.

At the bus stop Imogen smiled at a large woman loaded down with two enormous wicker shopping baskets. 'Excuse me, can you please tell me which buses go past Hamilton Harbour?' she asked shyly.

The woman beamed. 'Sure, they all do sweetpie. The only thing you need to look out for is this stripe on top of the pole,' she informed her, pointing to it. 'If it's pink, it means the buses that stop here are going to Hamilton. If it's blue, it means they're all going *away from* Hamilton.'

Imogen could only admire the simplicity of the system, and thanked her. Just then a bus came around the corner, and she got on, helping her fellow passenger with her baskets.

Morgan, watching this friendly gesture, smiled. Not quite such a spoilt brat as all that then. The thought pleased him far more than he'd have liked. It was one thing to be hooked, but it was another thing entirely to be fooled. Nevertheless, he had to admit, she surely was a creature of contrasts.

A few minutes later, Imogen felt a tap on her shoulder and looked around. 'This is the harbour just coming up, sweetpie.'

As she emerged into the bright sunlight, she clutched her red leather bag closer to her. Not because she suspected pickpockets so much, but simply out of nerves. Today she was entering the lion's den, and she wished she was wearing chain mail.

She didn't see the Jaguar which pulled to a halt near a stand of palms, or the tall figure which emerged and followed her down the pavement. Which was probably just as well.

She stopped to people-watch for a few moments. Everything about Bermuda pleased her. Perhaps it was the sunshine that did it! Hearing with delight the clip-clopping of horses, she turned to watch a horse-drawn carriage coming towards her. The inevitable tourist couple sat behind the smartly liveried driver. Everywhere she looked were little scooters, which were a popular item for hire with the tourists, along with ubiquitous bicycles. She strolled leisurely, pausing at a café to buy a delicious freshly made lemon-and-lime ice. Then, telling herself not to be such a coward, she found a board with a big map of the local area on it and quickly worked out the route to where she wanted to go. Despite her self-administered pep-talk, however, her feet were dragging just a bit as she stepped off the road and down a short incline to a large jetty. There she walked determinedly under an arch which bore the logo 'DAX DIVING'.

Behind her, Morgan Dax felt himself stiffen. He'd had a sneaking suspicion for the last few minutes where she must be heading, and as she stepped into his home turf, he smiled wolfishly. If she hoped to find him at home, she was going to be in for a disappointment. And he couldn't think why else she was here – unless she suddenly felt an urgent need to learn scuba diving!

No doubt after their run-in at the ball she'd decided to play nice and make up. It was a smart move after all; Elizabeth often turned to him for advice, as she must have found out by now, and it wouldn't pay her to make an enemy of the man with so much influence over her aunt.

He would have been surprised, therefore, to note the look of relief on Imogen's face when the guy in the small reception office told her that the 'boss' wasn't in.

'I was wondering, really, how hard it is to learn to dive,' Imogen smiled and lied with equal charm. The small office was pleasantly air-conditioned, and decorated with colourful posters depicting coral reefs, octopuses, starfish, and happy snorkellers, pointing thumbs up to the camera.

'Oh, it's easy, really. Of course, a good basic course is always recommended. Here at Dax Diving we run classes for absolute beginners to certificate level.'

Imogen smiled again and leaned amiably on the counter. It had the effect of pressing her breasts just a little more prominently against the gauzy material of her dress. The man behind the counter, a blond, bronzed beach-boy type, returned the smile and very firmly kept his eyes fixed to hers.

Well at least Morgan Dax trained his staff well, Imogen thought wryly. 'I dare say all you divers have certificates coming out of your ears?'

The young man laughed. 'Oh yes, ma'am. Mr Dax hires nothing but the best.' He reached for the large ledger in front of him. 'What did you have in mind? Snorkelling?'

Imogen shrugged, glanced around the empty office, and then back to the blond beach boy again. 'Well, to be honest, I'm a little bit scared. A friend of mine was over here a short while ago, and he told me a diving instructor drowned. Is that true?'

She saw the man's face close down and knew that this wasn't going to be easy. Just like nobody encouraged talk about the plane crash, so nobody wanted to talk about a fatal drowning. It was bad for everyone's business, and Dax Diving's business most of all.

'I'm afraid so, yes,' he said. 'But the diver in question ignored the company rules.'

Imogen felt herself bridle instantly on Robbie's behalf, and quickly forced the angry words she wanted to say back down. Besides, she knew Robbie never *had* paid much attention to rules, anyway.

'Really? Like what?' She opened her big blue eyes a bit wider and leaned just a little further forward.

The beach boy glanced around nervously. Luckily he didn't spot his boss, who was now standing behind a large green bush, wishing that the door was open so that he could hear what was going on inside. He'd expected her to emerge long before this. Just what was she doing in there? He was torn between a desire to walk in and confront her, and the instinctive feeling he had that it would be wiser to play a waiting game.

Inside, the young man was succumbing to the big blue eyes. 'Well, for a start, Mr Dax has a strict eight-hour-per-day limit for his instructors. Any more than that and he considers it far more likely they'll get tired or make mistakes. Legally, they can dive for longer than that, but Mr Dax always puts safety first.'

A regular Boy Scout, Imogen thought sourly, but was careful to keep her expression interested and approving.

'But this diver did longer hours?' she prompted. It sounded like Robbie, she had to admit.

'Yeah, he sure did. Not that he wasn't good, mind. One of the best in fact,' the young man added.

With a pang, Imogen wondered if he and her brother had been friends. Robbie was the type who made friends easily. And his easy-going attitude to life earned him his fair share of hero-worshippers from the younger, more naive element, who tended to regard him as a sort of lifestyle guru.

‘Even so, I wouldn’t have thought that would make much difference. Especially if he was as good as you say,’ she said, allowing her voice to become disbelieving.

The blond youngster shrugged. ‘He was also moonlighting. And that really is against the rules.’

Imogen felt herself stiffen, and forced herself to relax. ‘Oh? With another company, you mean?’

‘Nah, nothing like that. Robbie was the sort of guy to land on his feet, know what I mean?’

Imogen smiled and nodded. Oh yes, she knew what he meant.

‘Well, there’s this guy called Tony Jackson,’ he confided, relaxing enough to start chatting freely now. ‘He’s this big millionaire playboy type who comes to the islands about four months out of every year. Anyway, he took up diving in a big way and wanted a diving buddy who knew the ropes, so Robbie went for it. And got it. Course, being Robbie, he made sure that he kept his job here as well. He could hardly pay his tabs at the Beach Hut if he didn’t.’

‘The Beach Hut?’ Imogen echoed softly.

‘It’s a bar up past Two Rock Passage. It’s right on the beach, and has a thatched roof and everything. Real popular with the tourists. Robbie liked it because he could, er . . .’ He suddenly stuttered to a halt and went so red that Imogen laughed.

‘Pick up women there?’ she hazarded with a laugh.

He laughed too, glad she wasn’t offended. She was some looker. If he could just angle an invitation to go out for a drink with her, wouldn’t the guys’ eyes pop out of their heads if he walked in with this babe on his arm!

‘Yeah, he was a bit of a ladies’ man,’ he admitted.

‘So how did he die, exactly?’ Imogen asked, and realised at once that she’d gone too far as she saw him both mentally and physically pull away.

He straightened and fiddled with the pen. ‘Oh, you know. He must have misjudged the amount of diving time he had left. He just ran out of oxygen. But nothing like that can ever happen in our lessons or guided tours,’ he reassured her. 'And if diving isn't for you,' he segued smoothly, no doubt remembering that he was here to drum up business for his employer, 'have you ever thought about taking a glass-bottomed boat up to Stovell Bay? There's a shipwreck there and it's very popular. Our boats go all over the place,' he added, thrusting some leaflets into her hand.

Imogen, knowing that she'd got all she could from him, smiled warmly and thanked him for his time. He watched her walk out of the office and gave an unhappy sigh. He should have asked her for a date.

A moment or two later the door opened and he stood up just a little bit straighter, as everyone tended to when the boss was around. Not because he was an ogre or anything; in fact, most of his employees, especially the divers, called him by his first name. But you just couldn't help but be aware of the man's authority whenever he was about. Not that the boss himself traded on it.

'The woman who was just in,' Morgan began without preamble, surprising the booking clerk a little, who was used to a more amiable greeting from him. 'What did she want?' he demanded.

The booking clerk looked uneasy. 'Well, sir, I think she was just browsing. I tried to sell her the snorkelling classes, but she seemed very nervous of diving, so I gave her the glass-bottomed boat leaflets instead.'

Morgan's eyes narrowed. 'What made you think she was nervous of diving?'

'Well, sir, she'd heard about Robbie's accident. I think it put her off.'

He mentioned Robbie Dacres tentatively. Everyone knew that Morgan Dax had taken his drowning hard. Even after it emerged about Robbie's moonlighting and extra hours. Morgan, everyone agreed, was a good boss – one of the best. Nobody blamed him for the tragedy, but he'd been grim-faced for weeks after the accident.

'I see,' he said thoughtfully, and suddenly realising the young lad was looking miserable, he smiled. 'It's not your fault, Dwayne.' Looking around, he added, 'Things are quiet, eh?'

'Only because all the boats are out, sir. And the divers.'

'That's what I like to hear. What time's the last boat in? I was thinking of doing some diving myself later on. Ask Mac if he's free to be buddy when he comes in, would you?'

'Yes, sir.'

Morgan nodded and stepped outside, a scowl instantly replacing the smile on his face. Along the harbour road he could see her entrancing figure walking back to the bus stop. Just what was she up to now? What possible interest could she have in the silly, greedy, ultimately tragic Robbie Dacres?

As he walked slowly back to his Jag, Morgan could only think of one thing. She was digging up dirt on him. Trying to find something with which to blackmail him into obedience. No doubt she assumed that he didn't get to be as big as he was without getting his hands dirty, and if she could only find something on him, she'd be safe. Morgan smiled, without humour. If she was out for dirt, she was going to have a hard, fruitless search.

'You're obviously playing for keeps, Isadora Van Harte,' he said softly to the disappearing figure above him. 'Not to mention playing dirty. Very dirty.'

The thought, he had to admit, excited him. It was like being stalked by a delicious tigress. Spitting and growling now, but one day he'd hear her purr!

He slowly walked back to his car and got in, sitting inside thoughtfully. The inquest into Robbie Dacres had fully exonerated Dax Diving, as he'd always known it would. The diving equipment Dacres had been using had been checked thoroughly, and had passed all the accident investigators' guidelines. And Robbie had been diving alone, a strict no-no, as any diver would tell you. Add to that the fact that he'd taken out one of Dax's small powerboats without permission, and you had a perfect recipe for death by misadventure.

No, little Miss Gold-digger would find no joy in past scandals.

But she'd given him a good idea. He slowly began to smile. Two could play at this dirty little game of hers.

* * *

Elizabeth looked up and smiled as a shadow fell over her reclining garden chair. With Morgan's tall frame leaning over her, she said softly, 'Morgan, how nice! Averil was just in this morning. You can give her a book she wanted to borrow and forgot to take.'

'I'll do that,' Morgan said, stretching his large frame elegantly out on the lawn beside her. He was wearing the usual shorts and T-shirt, nevertheless managing to look as if he'd just stepped out of an important all-male club. 'How are you, Elizabeth? No more attacks?'

Elizabeth smiled gently. 'How you all fuss! You're as bad as that doctor of mine. I'm fine. Having Isadora around the house has given me a whole new interest in life. We're going to the theatre tonight.'

'Don't overdo it,' he said at once, smiling as Elizabeth gave him a speaking glance.

'I'm not in my grave yet, young man,' she said reprovingly. And added, apropos of nothing, 'She's such a lovely girl, my niece. Don't you think?'

'Sure. She could be a model,' he said flatly.

Elizabeth smiled, not at all fooled. 'Oh, I didn't mean that so much, although she is, of course, very beautiful. No, I meant her nature. She has a kind of patience and humanity that most young women these days never seem to cultivate,' she surprised Morgan greatly by saying. And wondered, to herself, how her house guest had come by it. Nursing a sick relative perhaps. Or getting over a broken heart. Or had she simply had the good fortune to be born with it?

'I can't say as I'd noticed,' Morgan said drolly. Nevertheless, he felt a touch uneasy. Elizabeth was nobody's pushover. She was niceness personified, but he'd long since come to realise that she had a sharp mind, and a good, experience-based ability to judge character. But this time it had to be letting her down. Didn't it?

Just then, Grace plodded out onto the shady veranda. 'Your bridge ladies are here, Miss Elizabeth,' she called gaily.

Elizabeth sighed and put her book to one side and Morgan rose to his feet quickly to help her up. Elizabeth twinkled up at him. She liked big, strong men. If she'd been younger . . .

As it was, she thought she'd leave him to Isadora.

They walked into the cool marble hall and greeted a gaggle of blue-rinsed ladies. 'I'll just nip into the library and get the book Averil wanted. What was it?' Morgan asked.

'*Swallows and Amazons*,' Elizabeth said. 'She said she'd read it once as a child and wanted to again.'

Morgan raised her old, gnarled hand to his lips and kissed it. His eyes twinkled bedevilment over her knuckles. He straightened. 'Ladies,' he said to Elizabeth's friends, before she gathered the twittering, admiring women into the study, where the table was all set up for bridge.

They played for money, and Elizabeth, as everyone knew, was a demon player. Morgan, who'd only ever sat in on one of their bridge afternoons once, had found himself fleeced for over a thousand dollars – and had promptly told them that if he wanted to gamble thereafter he'd fly to Nassau!

Once he was alone, he walked to the library and retrieved the book his sister wanted. Then, opening the door once more as stealthily as he could, he glanced out. Grace was nowhere to be seen. Morgan and Averil were both such constant visitors to the house that they more or less had the run of the place, and Grace certainly wouldn't have considered it necessary to show him out.

Feeling guilty, he crossed the hall and down one long, picture-bedecked corridor. He found the guest bedroom easily enough, and as he stepped into the room he glanced around uneasily.

It was one thing to play Miss Isadora Van Harte at her own manipulative little game, but another thing entirely to feel comfortable about it. Nevertheless, he did a quick check of the room. There was no correspondence in the little Edwardian knee-hole writing bureau. But her selection of books from Elizabeth's famously extensive library was surprising – Leigh Hunt – a poet he'd never really favoured, Ernest Hemingway, Trollope and an Agatha Christie. Quite an eclectic taste!

In point of fact, Imogen had only begun to appreciate literature after starting work at St Bede's, when she began to spend her lunchtimes in the college library.

Quickly, Morgan passed over the books and went on to her dressing table. The usual cosmetics, but not as many, he noticed with surprise, as his sister normally used. And only a single vial of perfume. Curiouser and curiouser.

When he got to her wardrobe he realised at once that all the clothes were brand new, and for a moment he was angry. Trust her to waste no time in fleecing her aunt. But then he realised that she must have lost everything – all her luggage, her passport, everything – in the crash.

He was about to close the wardrobe door when he noticed, hung at the back, an obviously ruined, saltwater-stained jacket. He felt a frisson of fear snake up his back as he realised that she must have been wearing it when the plane went down. And, for the first time, he began to seriously understand the trauma of what she must have gone through. And how lucky she'd been to survive.

To think that she might have died.

That he'd never have met her. Never have seen her under the moonlight, breathtaking and challenging, with clematis petals in her hair.

He held the jacket thoughtfully in his hand, and heard something in the pocket rustle. With a jolt of excitement, he drew out a wrinkled but now dry envelope.

A letter! And one, moreover, that she thought either important enough, or at least recent enough, to keep in her pocket.

He slowly extracted the stiffened pieces of paper from the envelope, reluctant to unfold them. He'd never before read anybody's private mail. But something, some portent, told him that this would be a vital clue. It might, in fact, hold the key to the mystery that was Isadora Van Harte.

Slowly, he began to read.

* * *

At that moment, Imogen was sitting on a padded bar stool at the Beach Hut, drinking something tasty but non-alcoholic from a real coconut shell. As the employee at Dax Diving had told her, it really was on the beach, had a thatched roof, and was a popular spot for tourists. Already three different men had tried to pick her up, but now the message seemed to be getting across, and she was glad to have a moment alone with the busy bartender.

'Someone told me that a guy used to come here,' she began, somewhat clumsily and impossibly vague.

'Yeah?' The bartender, who sported a very broad New York drawl, couldn't have sounded less interested.

'Yes, he was a diver. You know, taught the tourists and stuff. I heard later that he died.'

The bartender, a rather washed-out, thin, middle-aged man, suddenly looked more interested. 'Good-looking, dark-haired feller? Yeah, I heard about him. He used to be in here all the time. A real hit with the ladies. Always out for a quick buck. Heard his air ran out.'

Imogen managed not to wince. 'From the way his sister talked, I got the impression she thought there was foul play.'

The bartender cocked his head to one side. Something about his spurious interest made her feel sick. 'Yeah? Never heard nothing like that myself. Yeah, yeah all right. Bacardi coming up,' he yelled to one of his customers, who was getting fed up waiting for his drink.

Imogen watched him wander further down to the bar and serve some drinks, but wasn't surprised when he eventually made his way back to her. 'So, what you doing in Bermuda?' he asked.

'Me? Oh, just a holiday, you know. I mean, I never knew the man myself. It was tragic and all that, but you can't let sad stories ruin your fun, can you?' She forced herself to sound bright and uncaring.

'Too true, doll, too true. 'Sides, the guy wasn't worth crying over. He was a bum, ya know? Always boasting about getting rich. The last time I saw him in here, he was spinning some gal a tale about buying a yacht and going around the world in it. Like he already had the money in the bank, ya know?'

Imogen again fought back a wince. Sailing the world in his own luxury yacht had always been Robbie's dream.

'The fantasy-dwelling type was he?' she forced herself to ask, followed by a careless laugh.

'That's him. Though come to think of it,' the barman, who'd been half-heartedly rubbing down the bar with a dirty cloth, paused his rubbing and stared thoughtfully out to sea, 'that last night he was higher than usual. You know, talking a lot bigger. It wasn't "Someday I'm gonna do this or that", but more like "Hey, I've arrived. I'm a big shot now." That sort of boasting. You know?'

Imogen didn't. But she thought it was significant. Very significant.

Oh, Robbie, Robbie, she thought sadly, what on earth did you do? And if you had come into some money how did you get it? And who from? Where is it now?

And did you get killed because of it?

* * *

In her bedroom, Morgan Dax eagerly scanned the letter. It began, 'Dear I', and, he quickly turned to the last page, ended, 'Love R.'

A love letter? Somehow, the thought filled him with distaste and anger. But as he read he quickly realised that it was definitely no kind of love letter. More like a postcard-type missive you wrote to your friends back home.

Then he began to frown. The letter began to get more peculiar. He noticed too how some words were written in darker ink, but thought the effect must have been caused by its immersion in the sea, especially with some of them being slightly blurred.

When he read the part about something being rotten in the state of Bermuda he stopped and read it again. But there was no clue as to what the writer of the letter meant by that. And yet something about it disturbed him deeply.

Slowly he folded the letter back into the envelope, slipped it into the jacket pocket and put the garment away at the back of the wardrobe where he'd found it.

Who was R? And where was he now? Was Isadora secretly meeting him? It now seemed possible that there was more to her coming to the island than simply to get her hooks into Elizabeth's money.

He left the bungalow and walked back to his car a thoughtful and disturbed man. Suddenly, he was not at all sure that he understood little Miss Isadora Van Harte even half so well as he thought he did. And as he drove the car to his corporate offices on Happy Valley Road, he decided it was high time he got to know her better.

Much better.

SEVEN

Ellis Reynolds walked across the large white expanse that was the main room of his penthouse and opened the French doors leading onto the balcony. Outside, Devonshire Dock lay off to his right, and above him, gulls wheeled in the darkening sky, crying out at the setting of the sun.

It had been a wonderful day.

First of all the delight of a new experience – parascending. Then lunch with Averil Dax, where he'd finally, officially, introduced himself. Watching her eat crab cakes and salad had been as much a pleasure as floating in the air had been. Then the walk on the beach, holding her hand. It was amazing how easy and comfortable they'd felt together. She'd told him all about her childhood – about growing up in Boston, about being rich, even a little about her family's plans to marry her off to a 'suitable' candidate.

Then it had been his turn, and he'd deliberately made her laugh, telling her something about growing up in London. The wheezes he'd pulled in school. Oxford.

She'd been fascinated by Oxford, and he'd promised to take her there one day. It had seemed the most natural thing in the world to say it. He'd meant it.

And she'd known he meant it.

Even now, after he'd dropped her off at the big house she shared with her brother, he knew she was probably humming away, perhaps taking a bath, thinking with pleasure about the future.

Only now, as he leaned against the balcony and looked out across the ocean, did Ellis admit to himself that there would probably never be an Oxford. Not for them. Not once she knew why he was here . . .

Ellis sighed and ran a hand through his silvery hair. His green eyes narrowed as the sun slowly sank towards the horizon. As beautiful and spectacular as it was, he couldn't help but view it as a wasted sunset. He should have stayed with her even longer. Invited her out to dinner maybe. Driven her to Gibbs Hill, the highest point on the island, so that they could watch the sun go down together.

He turned abruptly from the natural cabaret in front of him and instead reached for his phone. It was time he called Justin: his partner.

He'd met Justin Smythe-Johns in Oxford. They'd been next-door neighbours in one of the genteelly broken-down residences of the college, and had quickly become friends, proving the old adage that opposites really do attract. Justin was the son of a baronet, raised by a nanny, an ex-Etonian and about as far removed from the wildly ambitious boy from poverty-stricken East End London as it was possible to get. Whereas Ellis, who saw his scholarship-funded Oxford education as his one chance in life, slogged hard and earned a first in Politics and Economics, Justin barely scraped a third in Modern History. And whereas Ellis had plans to set up his own company and build his own empire, Justin mournfully prepared to go back to rural Hertfordshire to learn the ropes and eventually take over the running of his family's estates.

It had been Ellis who, with his usual determination and persuasiveness, had more or less bullied Justin into throwing in his lot with him. To invest all of the money from his paternal grandmother that became his at the age of twenty-three into Reynolds-Smythe, Diamond Merchants. It had been a glamorous enough field of endeavour to appeal to the romantic in Justin, and he'd long since learned to trust in Ellis's grasp both of economics and the way the cut-throat world of business worked.

It had helped, naturally, that his well-heeled family had thrown a collective fit. Justin was at the age to be rebellious, and his kith and kin had predicted disaster. Ellis, they insisted, was a no-good cockney crook, who'd take his money, squander it and disappear.

Justin didn't think so. And Justin had been right.

Not that anything had come easy. It hadn't. The high-risk, high-flying world of diamond dealing was a tight-knit and highly controlled community. And, for a while, Reynolds-Smythe was a strictly small-time outfit.

Ellis, determined to be careful as well as innovative, cannily began in a way that would alarm no one. Not Justin, not his sceptical family, and not the big boys in the diamond world. In short, he began by setting up in the industrial diamond business. Boart, as the stones were called, were only worth about $2 a carat on a good day, but there was steady money to be made, and Reynolds-Smythe made it. A reputation for trustworthiness and stability was tenderly nurtured. And, as Ellis knew only too well, they had an apprenticeship which needed to be served.

He'd chosen the field of diamonds because he was convinced of their long-term potential. But he also knew he had to learn an awful lot as he went along.

And learn he did.

With Justin providing the blue-blooded pedigree and his background of solid, old-time money, they were able to soothe the older, more stick-in-the-mud firms and quickly win over that section of the world they'd chosen to make their own. But with Ellis's undoubted business acumen and go-getting personality, they also pleased the new boys, the risk-takers, the movers and shakers. Not surprisingly, therefore, Reynolds-Smythe soon outgrew boart, even though it had given them a firm, well-funded financial base.

But Ellis wasn't satisfied with merely doing all right, and had shown no hesitation in moving into the more challenging field of gemstone-quality diamonds. And he was a natural, the equipment of his trade becoming as familiar to him as the back of his hand – the tiny scales, the scoops for easy movement of gems, the loupe (the miniature telescope-like instrument he viewed stones through to assess their quality) – everything came easy to him. Even the expensive cutters they employed had to admit he handled calibrators, rulers, pincers and microscopes as if he'd been doing it for years. As if he'd learned it at his father's knee, as they had.

Of course, cutting was a whole different game altogether, but Ellis was determined to at least understand and become knowledgeable about that too. For months, he'd taken every opportunity that came up to watch Albert Fishman, their chief cutter, working. Fishman – at first reluctantly, but then as he got to know his new employer better, with outright enthusiasm – began to actively teach him how to 'feel' stones. To know which diamond, resembling nothing so much as a rather dull pebble, would cut up into a multifaceted, sparkling gem, and which stones would crumble, or produce poor-quality colour.

Ellis, as well as setting up markets, travelling the globe, buying and selling and building up Reynolds-Smythe's reputation, also saw how to cut a 'window'. This process allowed a skilled cutter to cut a tiny piece into a diamond, in order to assess its colour and quality. And while he was doing this, Justin did his bit. His became a familiar face in the Bursa, situated in Ramat Gan in Tel Aviv, the Israeli centre being one of the most important diamond centres in the world.

Both Justin and Ellis were members of IADD, the International Association of Diamond Dealers, and right now Ellis had ambitious plans to buy into a business consortium in Angola where alluvial riverbeds (the kind that produced diamonds) had been discovered.

Of course, they had enemies. They were growing bigger and more influential every day. You couldn't do that without attracting unwanted attention. And the price-fixing cartel that practically ran all aspects of the diamond business had made their presence, and what they expected of Reynolds-Smythe, very clear indeed.

But Ellis had no intention of bucking the big boys, preferring to get into bed with them. The result of all this careful planning, mixed with knowledge, natural ability and the desire to take carefully calculated risks, meant that Reynolds-Smythe was now a major player. They were based in Amsterdam, but Ellis was about to move them to Antwerp, for he considered the Belgian city to be the growing centre of the diamond world.

Justin, of course, agreed with him. But then he would: Justin had seen his original investment rise like a rocket, and knew when he was on to a good thing. Even his family had started calling Ellis by his first name (and not 'that cockney crook') and inviting him regularly to weekend parties and dinners at the baronial pile.

It had all been going so well that Ellis had almost been expecting a setback of some kind. But he'd been as surprised and stunned as Justin by the form it had finally taken. As dealers, they regularly sent 'envelopes' of stones by courier to various other dealers, buyers and middlemen. For years they'd done so without a hitch. But then, three months ago, one of their shipments had been hit. An armed gang had got away with over a quarter of a million pounds' worth of cut stones. Any diamond company had to keep at least £600,000 of stones in stock so it wasn't a death-blow by any means. And, of course, they were insured.

The police had investigated it thoroughly, and none of the courier staff or staff at Reynolds-Smythe were considered to be suspects in the theft. Consequently, the insurance company had agreed to pay up, not wanting to lose such a good customer or alienate the diamond trade.

To Justin, it had just been 'one of those things'. It happened to more or less everyone in the business at some time or other. An occupational hazard, in fact. Since no one had been hurt in the raid, he'd quickly shrugged it off.

Not so Ellis. Ellis had fumed at people in his employ being terrified with sawn-off shotguns. And chafed at the fact that others had stolen his property. Stones which belonged to him! Also, he strongly felt that he couldn't let them get away with it. He knew that if he could successfully recover the stones then it would send a much-needed warning shot across the bows of other potential thieves. Not to mention the fact that Reynolds-Smythe would bathe in the kudos that would come their way from their rivals. And the publicity alone would ensure them more business, especially if Reynolds-Smythe gained a reputation as a firm not to be messed with.

So he'd taken the decision to hire a highly rated, exorbitantly expensive team of private investigators, headed by an ex-CID officer called Charlie Hassett. Charlie had told him straight – it was no good going after the perpetrators. They'd have split up and been long gone. No, the way to find his stones was to find the fence. And Ellis, trusting his judgement of men, had decided to give Charlie his head.

It had taken him over a month. It had cost the firm thousands. Justin had howled, but had quickly backed down when he saw Ellis was adamant. Justin was not about to rock the boat. He'd gone from potential estate-farm manager in dull Hertfordshire to high-flying diamond dealer jetting off to South Africa, Israel and Latin America, because he'd gone along with Ellis Reynolds. He liked sipping champagne at ambassadors' residences and having women fawn over him because of his endearing but annoying habit (to Ellis, anyway!) of providing them with little diamond trifles. They had, in many ways, an ideal partnership that both were confident would stand the test of time.

Now Ellis punched in Justin's telephone number, not even thinking of the time difference which would have his partner getting out of bed. Eventually his sleepy voice answered. 'Yeah? What the hell time is it?' The muffled complaint was said with an upper-crust twang that always made Ellis smile.

'Justin, it's me.'

In his Amsterdam house, a tall, thin dwelling typical of the city, Justin opened his eyes a bit wider. 'Ellis! How's it going? Seen any mysterious triangles?'

'Clown! Listen, I just wanted to keep you updated. I think Charlie hit the nail right on the head.'

'You've seen Jackson?' Justin asked sharply.

'Yes, I've seen him,' Ellis said grimly. 'And he's just like Charlie described. A reptile. If he hasn't got our stones I'll be very surprised.'

In his bed, Justin grimaced. 'Be careful, OK? You read the dossier they gave us on this creep. He's a sewer rat.'

'Oh, he's that all right.'

Charlie had provided him with a complete lowdown on Tony Jackson, aka Francis De Corvier, real name Vincenzo Aiello. The police in several countries were convinced that he was a high-class fence, with a stolen artwork venture and a money-laundering operation usually only reserved for the Mafia. That Jackson had managed to stay independent was another thing that warned all who knew anything about crime not to treat him lightly.

'So, what exactly are you planning on doing now?' Justin asked, not unreasonably. He was nervous to have his partner so far away, and in such a dangerous situation.

'I've been asking around about him,' Ellis mused, sitting on the long white leather couch and staring thoughtfully out across the darkening sky. 'He does what you'd expect of a lounge lizard – partying, dating pretty girls,' his voice gritted just a little at this, 'and gambling. But one thing struck me as odd. A little while ago he got the diving bug.'

Justin, who liked to swim, ski and dive too (like most well-rounded, upper-crust Englishmen), was unconvinced. 'Nothing suspicious in that, old chap, I assure you.'

Ellis smiled. 'But our boy is not a born sportsman like you, Justin. Take my word for it: for our friend Jackson to go to all the trouble of getting wet, he must have had a damned good reason for it. Besides, if he'd done it for his image, of which he's very proud I might add, he'd have gone about it differently. You know, made a big show of it. Invited a magazine in to do a "playboy at play" kind of article. But he didn't. He sneaked around. He bought a second-hand boat. He hired a no-hoper beach-bum type to buddy him. Hardly "Island Playboy Meets the Coral Reef".'

There was a short silence as Justin digested all this. 'So what are you saying?' he asked finally. 'That he's hidden the stones underwater somewhere?'

'Why not?' Ellis mused aloud. 'He's got to be a genius at finding hiding places for his caches or else the cops would have found them out by now. They've certainly stuck enough search-and-seizure orders on him in the past, but have only come up empty-handed.'

'Well, if he *has* hidden them under the sea, what hope have you got of finding them?' Justin asked reasonably. 'That is, if he hasn't sold them on already.'

Ellis sighed. 'Don't be such a defeatist! I'm going to get closer to him. See if I can't find something out.'

'Be careful!' Justin's sharp voice, tinged with unmistakable fear, came quickly over the line again.

'Don't worry. I have no intention of turning up knifed in some alley somewhere,' Ellis said grimly. He'd taken a quick but intensive course in self-defence, run by an ex-SAS major that Charlie Hassett had introduced him to. The things that the ex-soldier had taught Ellis to do, if it came down to a gutter-type fight for his life, would have made the civilised Justin's hair stand on end. They talked for a little while longer and then hung up.

As Ellis walked back out onto the balcony, and watched a sky now full of stars, resembling the diamonds that had become his way of life, he sighed. He hadn't told Justin about Averil Dax. But then, what could he say? Oh, by the way, I've fallen in love. But no, I won't be marrying her.

She's Tony Jackson's girlfriend.

* * *

Ironically, Tony Jackson himself was also studying the night sky. He was on his yacht, *Sea Siren*, and had a Scotch on the rocks in one hand and a semi-naked girl stretched out beneath the other.

He couldn't remember her name. He was in a bad mood. He, too, was thinking how the stars were like diamonds. Diamonds which had once, briefly, been his.

When he'd heard about the diamond robbery in London, he'd half-guessed that he'd soon be called upon to fence them, which he had, two days later. An acquaintance of his who had a weakness for gems was in the market, and people in the know knew that he preferred to deal with Tony Jackson.

At first, it had all gone as sweetly as honey. An anonymous man had flown in and met an anonymous boat that couldn't be traced to either of them. On this very yacht, Tony had then swapped cash for the stones. He'd already thought of a brilliant place to hide them where no customs official or Interpol cop could ever find them.

The only thing was, he needed help.

And so he'd scouted around, and learned about Robbie Dacres. Robbie, with no family to speak of, no ties, no cares. Greedy, amiable Robbie, who taught him how to dive. Who knew enough about the world to 'buddy' him with no questions asked. Robbie, who took him to shipwrecks, both important and obscure.

It was in one such obscure place, a wreck of a 1950s fishing trawler, that Tony had found his ideal hiding place. Diamonds were so amenable. They didn't rust. Didn't rot. Didn't do anything except sparkle. He knew his friend expected to wait a while for the fuss to die down, and Tony knew he'd be suspected. What better place, then, to temporarily stash the stones than in miles and miles of anonymous blue ocean? In an undistinguished shipwreck, beneath an undistinguished anchor.

And so he had collected the stones from his safe one fine evening and gone diving with Robbie. He'd thought he'd been so clever. He'd made no great show of where he wanted to dive, only casually mentioned the fishing boat wreck once they'd put out to sea. And once down, he'd been deliberately lazy, letting Robbie get well ahead of him before transferring the small sack of stones from under his weight-belt. What's more, he'd been positive that Dacres hadn't seen him hide the stones. His back had been fully turned, and he'd been inspecting a starfish at the time.

The girl stirred, murmured something, then fell asleep again. She was drunk.

He'd almost resigned himself to the loss, but then he'd heard that Dacres' sister was coming to Bermuda. He had spies and contacts everywhere – including the airport. And once again, he was in danger. What if Dacres had told her about him? But then she'd died so obligingly in the crash. The only thing that gnawed at him was the frustrating thought that her brother might have told her where the diamonds were hidden.

Now, he had to finally cut his losses and stop obsessing about them. But even so, he was out over $250,000. And he didn't like it. Not one little bit. Angrily, he finished his drink. Even worse, he was beginning to hear nasty little rumours that the firm that had lost the stones, Reynolds-Smythe, wasn't happy. That they were poking their noses in.

Now that really would be unwise, Tony thought, with a smile like a shark.

Very unwise indeed.

EIGHT

As promised, Elizabeth had set up a visit to the Botanical Gardens, and that morning they spent a leisurely hour or so as Imogen was introduced to all its many delights. Going in through the Berry Hill entrance, they'd already toured the cacti and the conifer collection and were walking up towards the aviary when Elizabeth suddenly smiled widely.

'How marvellous,' she enthused. 'Here's Morgan.'

Imogen felt her heart lurch, as if she'd just stepped into a lift which had descended without warning and far too fast. She turned, forcing a smile onto her face, and watched him loping across the large Camden lawn towards them.

He was wearing cut-off denim shorts, slightly frayed, at mid-thigh level. His long, tanned legs easily ate up the yards, and Imogen had the sensation of an approaching storm. Not that he looked dark-faced, or even menacing. It was just that she could actively feel a force of nature approaching her, and one which she instinctively wanted to shelter from. And yet, another part of her was determined to meet it head on.

A plain white T-shirt stretched across his chest and shoulders, delineating the lines of his muscles. His hair, in the slight breeze, moved off his forehead in motion to his steps. His eyes, dark-fire lasers, seemed to sweep across the terrain and penetrate her blood and sinew. Without warning, Imogen could feel her nipples start to tingle, and she quickly looked away.

Damn the man, was he going to show up *everywhere* she went?

Elizabeth, apparently, felt no such restraint. 'Morgan, lovely to see you again. Was Averil pleased with her book? Would you like to come back to our place for lunch?'

'Yes and yes please,' he said easily. 'Or perhaps I could tempt you ladies to lunch at the Lobster Pot with me?'

'Oh, I think you could twist our arms,' Elizabeth said, and laughed lightly. 'We were just going to see the birds.'

'Lovely,' Morgan said, looking straight at Imogen.

She was dressed in a mint-green dress made of a light, gauzy material, ideal for a warm, tropical day. Her hair was held back in a French pleat, and had looped down its length tiny, matching mint-green ribbons. She was wearing no make-up, he noticed, and for some reason that unsettled him. Most women he knew didn't have the confidence or the originality to go about with a bare face. The fact that this woman of all women should be so different set him on edge.

And her face was so lovely.

Elizabeth's eyes twinkled as she watched him gaze openly at her young companion, and after touring the aviary, the native and endemic plants and the arrowroot and fern collection, Elizabeth didn't have to feign tiredness.

Imogen noticed it first. 'Elizabeth, why don't we find a nice bench for you to sit on? You must be tired.'

'Well, dear, I wouldn't mind. But you two carry on. Morgan, you must show her the exotic house,' she added mischievously.

For some reason, this made Imogen blush, and a gentle, becoming wave of pink quickly enveloped her cheeks and throat. Morgan watched, fascinated. It had been a long time since he'd seen a woman blush.

Imogen cursed herself, and him, and this day, which had started out so nicely and without a hint of warning of the disasters to come. 'Oh, but surely you don't want to be left alone,' she demurred rapidly to Elizabeth, as they walked across Camden back towards the area of private residences where Hartelands was situated. They found a bench in between two bulb borders, shaded by a leafy tree which Imogen didn't recognise.

'Oh, I don't mind a bit,' Elizabeth said uncooperatively. 'It's so warm and lovely here. Besides, I like watching the butterflies. You two get along, and come back for me later. I'm holding you to that offer of lunch at the Lobster Pot, Morgan,' she added, smiling up at him.

Morgan grinned back. 'As if I'd dare renege.' His smile left his face as he turned back to Imogen. 'This way then,' he said, rather more abruptly than he'd intended.

'Yes, sir, right away, sir,' Imogen muttered under her breath, but both Elizabeth and Morgan caught it. Elizabeth quickly hid a smile by looking down at her feet, and Morgan scowled.

'So, how are you enjoying Bermuda?' he asked as they moved off, in an obvious effort to at least be pleasant. He'd come to the gardens on the off chance of meeting Elizabeth, and perhaps discovering a few titbits of information from her about her niece. Spotting them both together had seemed like too good an opportunity to pass up, but now he was not so sure.

He was having trouble keeping his eyes off her legs, which were long and slender and perfectly shaped. And the way the dark plait bounced against her back, almost reaching her curvaceous bottom. And the long dark lashes which kept sweeping down over her eyes. And the way she had of breathing, which seemed specifically designed to press her gently rounded breasts more firmly against the demure mint-green gauze.

'Oh, it's wonderful,' Imogen said, this time with real enthusiasm. The island had been working its magic on her ever since her terrifying arrival on it, as if determined to make it up to her for the tragedy and pain.

She still had nightmares about the crash, of course, and whenever she read something about it in the papers, she would still break down and cry for her fellow travellers.

And for Isadora most of all.

But she was healing, as was only natural, and Bermuda was her greatest remedy. 'It's a really lovely place. Like paradise. And Elizabeth has insisted I do nothing but sightsee, laze around the pool or go to her favourite beauty parlour,' she smiled gently. 'I'm having trouble convincing her it's high time it stopped.'

'Oh. Don't you like the decadent lifestyle?' he teased.

Imogen laughed. 'I'm not used to it, that's all.' And she was determined *not* to get used to it, if she possibly could. Already she was beginning to dread returning home, and she knew that after all this, her ordinary way of life would be unbearably dull unless she could keep her feet firmly on the ground now.

They were walking through the palm gardens and the dappled shade was a pleasant relief from the brightness of the day. Still barely 10:30, there weren't that many visitors yet, and Morgan, for one, was glad to have the place more or less to themselves.

He glanced across at her curiously. 'So your father never had *any* Van Harte money then?' he probed. That was strange. From what he'd gleaned from Elizabeth in the past, he'd got the distinct impression that her brother had been provided for – not with the fortune that he could have expected had the family not quarrelled with him, but at least a very comfortable settlement.

Imogen realised instantly that she'd boobed, and she swallowed a quickly rising lump of fear in her throat. From her own conversation with Isadora on the plane, she too had got the impression of someone who'd never wanted for anything.

'Well, we certainly never lived on this scale,' she spread her hands out to indicate the scenery around her and laughed hollowly (and, she suspected, unconvincingly). 'I mean, the island itself, living on Bermuda I mean, is a whole different way of life from anything else, isn't it?' she gabbled, desperately trying to paper over the cracks.

Morgan remembered his own first days on the island. How vastly different it had felt from his old life back in Boston, as luxurious and privileged as that had been. 'Yes, I suppose so,' he admitted. But even so, he knew she was hiding something. She was, he was rather pleased to note, a poor liar.

They bypassed the garden for the blind, and cut across towards the building that housed the exotic plants. 'You don't talk about your family much, do you?' Morgan, with all the skills of the great tactician he was, released the deadly little dart at the optimum moment, and watched her closely. He was in no mood to be merciful. In point of fact, he considered she had far too many advantages already for him to give her any leeway at all. He could almost feel her silken rope winding around him! Hell, it felt good.

Imogen, floored by the accusation, almost laughed out loud. For how *could* she talk about *her* family? She knew nothing about them! 'I don't want to upset Elizabeth by discussing it,' she said stiffly.

Morgan grunted, but he was now more convinced than ever that she was hiding something. And, like many men when issued a challenge, he simply couldn't resist it. But before he could ask another leading question, rigged with mines and pitfalls, she forestalled him.

'But what about you?' Imogen quickly turned the tables. 'I understand you live with your sister. Didn't we meet briefly at the ball?' She hoped her voice came out as light and casual as she'd intended. She was beginning to suspect she'd make a lousy actress!

'Averil? Yes,' he shrugged, and gave her a shortened version of his family history.

'So you wanted to strike out on your own?' she mused, when he'd finished. They stood aside at the entrance to the exotic house to let the doors open and a couple with a child in a pushchair pass through. They looked damp and wrung-out.

'Banking never really appealed to me,' Morgan explained, holding the door open for her. 'It was never rewarding enough.'

The moment they stepped in, it was like walking into a warm, wet, oxygen-depleted tent. Imogen gasped. All around her was exotic colour – towering, large-leafed plants with huge blooms. Butterflies and hummingbirds darted from plant to plant. A mock waterfall trickled a deceiving sound of cooling water throughout the display. But it was so enervating!

It was deserted, for the moment, and Imogen wasn't surprised that so many people preferred to give this exhibit a miss.

'Wow,' she said feelingly.

'Hm. An acquired taste, I think,' he agreed drolly.

But Imogen wasn't about to let him be sidetracked. She was determined to keep him talking, and then steer the conversation towards his diving schools. And Robbie.

'So what made you choose sports and leisure activities? For your company, I mean?' she asked, as they set off through the man-made jungle.

Morgan glanced down at her. Already his face was beaded with sweat, as was her own. There was one little bead of moisture on the tip of her nose which he wanted desperately to lick off. He shrugged his impressive shoulders and slowly led her towards the miniature waterfall.

'Oh, I always liked sports. People will always want to be active and creative, and with the trend towards leisure-related activities growing all the time, sports and leisure was an obvious choice. Besides, I've always loved diving, ever since I went away with my school at fourteen to the Caribbean. I got the bug,' he grinned, his sudden little-boy charm catching Imogen unawares.

She took a deep breath and dragged her mind back to business. It was difficult when there was a curl of dark-gold hair falling to his left eyebrow which she really wanted to brush back. 'And so from something as simple as that grew Dax Leisure?' she let her voice rise disbelievingly.

'That's right,' he confirmed, unabashed. 'The boats came first – water-skiing, parasailing, the cruises. Then the line of sportswear shops, then the diving schools.'

'But you like the diving schools best?'

'I suppose. They're not the biggest money earners though.'

'But you like diving,' she persisted, like a dog worrying a bone. 'Do you do much of it? Do you ever work as an instructor at the school itself?'

'Sometimes, if we're short-staffed.' He looked at her oddly, but she didn't heed the warning.

'Does that happen often?' she charged ahead.

Morgan paused on a plank bridge crossing a stream. A big powder-blue butterfly fluttered past him. Startled, Imogen watched it, and then looked back into his face. And discovered, with a jolt, that he was observing her closely. 'You seem very interested in the diving school,' he murmured dangerously. 'Is there anything specific you want to know?'

Imogen felt her pulse rate rocket. 'No, why should I?' she squeaked. 'It was you who said you had the diving bug. I was just being polite, asking you about it.' She shrugged an elegant shoulder and looked away nonchalantly. Damn, he was touchy! *And* he seemed able to see right through her.

Morgan's lips twisted into a semblance of a smile. 'It was just that I was down at the harbour the other day, and one of my staff said that you'd been in, asking questions. About a fatality,' he added flatly. He was tired of all this fencing. He wanted a straightforward answer for once, and as he watched her lovely profile, he saw her pale.

'Yes. Elizabeth told me about it,' she finally whispered. 'We were talking about how close you and your sister are to her, and from that she got on to the trouble you'd had with one of your divers recently. That she'd hated to see how upset you were about it.' Imogen felt her throat drying up more and more for every lie she told. It was a real struggle for her to finish. 'So when I was down at the harbour and saw your diving school, I thought I'd call in, you know, just to see what this diving business is all about, and we just got talking.'

She licked her paper-dry lips nervously. 'I didn't realise you kept tabs on me,' she added darkly, suddenly shooting him a suspicious look. She'd been so busy defending herself that she hadn't really taken in before just how suspicious his own behaviour was.

'What's wrong, Morgan?' she said softly, lifting her chin pugnaciously. 'Is there some reason you don't like people talking about the dead boy? Robbie something or other his name was, wasn't it?'

She knew she was playing a dangerous game now. If Morgan *did* have something to do with Robbie's death, then she was well and truly alerting him to the fact that someone was on to him. But now that she had him on the ropes, she just couldn't back away.

Morgan slowly began to shake his head. 'No, I have no problems with talking about him,' he said, his eyes nevertheless narrowing on her grimly. 'His name was Robbie Dacres. He came to the islands about a year or so ago. All his diving certificates were in order, so when he came looking for a job I had a couple of the lads take him out and check him over. He was good. Very good. He knew his theory as well as his practical.' He shrugged. 'So I hired him. And for the most part, everything went well.'

His voice became gruffer. 'So when the local police phoned me one night and told me that the body of one of my divers had been found I thought—' He broke off and sighed heavily, running a hand through his dampening hair. 'I thought there must have been some sort of a tragic accident. Perhaps one of the boats had overturned. It wasn't until the facts began to come out that I realised that it was due to negligence, not to accidental circumstances, that he'd died.'

Imogen forced herself not to think of Robbie but to concentrate on Morgan. He sounded sincere. He had the tight look of remembered pain creasing his face. But he could just be a marvellous actor, couldn't he?

'Yes, the man at your office told me about his diving alone,' she responded stiffly.

'But what was he doing out there on his own?' Morgan suddenly gritted, slamming his hands down on the bridge's railing in apparent frustration. 'That's what I can't understand. Robbie was no idiot – he knew the rules. He knew how dangerous it could be, going down alone. And how on earth did he come to run out of air? That just beggars belief. No diver, not even a novice, forgets to check his tanks.'

Imogen felt herself beginning to swell with hope. Surely if he were responsible for killing Robbie he wouldn't be bringing her attention to all the anomalies involved in it.

But all her happiness fled as he suddenly turned to look at her with open suspicion. 'Unless you know more about this than you're telling?' he grated accusingly.

Imogen stiffened. Her eyes grew wide. 'Me?' she squeaked. 'I wasn't even here.' Morgan slowly turned, leaning his back against the bridge, watching her. She felt as exposed as an insect under a microscope.

'No, you weren't here,' he admitted softly. 'But Robbie only came to Bermuda a year ago. Before that, he must have been somewhere else. Bournemouth, maybe? He was English, after all. I hear those southern English towns appreciate a certain type of man. A man like Robbie. A guy used to getting along on his looks.'

Suddenly he was remembering that letter of hers, kept in her jacket pocket, within easy reach. *Love* R. R for Robbie?

For her part, Imogen was lost. Bournemouth? What was he going on about? And then she realised that that was where the real Isadora had come from. And, yes, he was definitely implying that Robbie was some sort of gigolo. She almost laughed. Then, with her usual innate honesty, promptly wondered if it was so outlandish a suggestion after all? She could well understand her amoral brother thinking it nothing more than a lark to live off a lovestruck older woman. He might have done just that.

But Morgan had seen the glint of laughter in her eyes, and her reaction had been so far removed from the jealousy or anger he'd expected that he found himself longing to shake the truth out of her. If Robbie had been her lover, and she was here to find out about his death, why would the thought of his living off older women amuse her? Because she didn't believe it? Or because she just didn't care?

'I wouldn't know how Robbie Dacres got along in life,' Imogen responded to his taunts with a coolness that only fired his anger. 'Never having met the man,' she added, turning to look down dismissively into the water. It was easily her best performance so far.

The big powder-blue butterfly returned, settling briefly on her bare wrist, probing her skin for salt, and then fluttering off. Imogen watched it, enchanted. And the look of innocent pleasure on her face, after all his ugly thoughts about her, was Morgan's final undoing.

'Oh, this is ridiculous,' he snapped, making her head shoot around and towards him. 'Just what are you doing here, Isadora Van Harte?' He closed the gap between them with two steps and grasping the tops of her arms, spinning her around to face him. Imogen was forced to take a hasty step forward in order to regain her balance, and found herself trapped in his arms. The air, already soggy and hard to breathe, became almost suffocating.

She gasped.

'Are you just trying to get money out of Elizabeth? Is that what all this is about?' he demanded.

Imogen looked so shocked that for an instant, a wonderful, dizzying instant, he wanted to laugh out loud.

'No!' Imogen cried. 'Take advantage of Elizabeth? That wonderful woman? Just what kind of person do you think I am?' she snarled, and her hand shot back, ready to deliver a stinging blow to his face.

But she never delivered it. Because, suddenly, she realised that he didn't deserve it. She *was* taking advantage of Elizabeth. She was lying to her, and living under her roof under false pretences. Elizabeth really *did* need defending from her. And this man was doing just that. No matter what question marks still hung over his head as far as Robbie was concerned, she didn't doubt that he was genuinely fond of her aunt. No. Not her aunt. Elizabeth. She had to keep remembering that.

Morgan, unaware of her exact thoughts but fascinated by the play of emotions skittering across her expressive face, slowly looked from her hand, still raised above her and poised to strike, and then back to her face. Miserably, Imogen lowered her hand.

'I think,' she began, but wasn't allowed to finish her thought – namely, that they'd better go.

'You think too damned much,' Morgan growled instead, and pulled her towards him. Imogen had time only to take a quick, surprised breath, and then his lips were on hers. She felt her head swim, and this time it had nothing to do with the tropical atmosphere. She became aware of everything instantly. The chirping of a bird, somewhere above her, calling to its mate. A single drop of perspiration, snaking its way down her spine, tickling her. The sound of his breathing harmonising with her own.

The touch of his hands on her body. The scent of his aftershave. Every single tiny receptor and nerve ending in her lips, where they were pressed against his. The moisture of his tongue against hers. His fingers splaying more urgently against her back. The way her nipples, crushed against his chest, began to throb and ache. The sudden weakness in her knees.

And then it was over. He pulled away, a small sound, not quite a sigh, not quite a moan, leaving his lips as they left hers. Her eyes, which had remained locked open in surprise, watched his as they feathered open.

They were so close she could see his black pupils dilate in the dark-chocolate irises of his eyes. She saw his nostrils flare, like those of a startled horse. Saw a look, almost of panic, cross his face. And then he was pushing her away.

He coughed, and shook his head. 'I shouldn't have done that,' he said roughly, aware that he was hardly acting like the mature man that he considered himself to be. Hell, it was only a kiss! He'd ended full-blown sexual relationships with less awkwardness than this. 'Please, forget I ever did that,' he added, only making it worse.

Imogen shook her head. 'I don't think I can,' she said, saying the first thing that came into her head. But she'd never been kissed like that before in her life. Not even Francis Dwyer, whom she'd thought she'd loved, had made her feel like that.

She swayed and reached for the bridge for support. It's the heat, she thought frantically. That's what it is. Once I get outside, into the fresh air, I won't feel so shattered. But even as she turned and stumbled blindly for the door, she knew it wasn't the heat. And she knew that she wouldn't forget that kiss. Not if she lived to be a hundred.

But what did it mean?

As the outdoor air hit her, and she walked, dazed, back towards the lawn and the waiting Elizabeth, she was forced to admit to herself that she knew exactly what it meant. Had always known what it meant. Right from the very first moment she'd set eyes on him in the hospital room.

Right from their first dance together.

But what could she do about it? She was in love with the man who might have killed her brother.

Was she supposed to be *happy* about that?

NINE

Ellis's MG roared to a growling halt outside the Elbow Beach hotel, and a valet quickly stepped forward. Ellis, dressed in a navy-blue suit, white shirt and maroon tie stepped out, walked around to the passenger door and opened it. The valet's attention quickly switched to the pair of shapely legs that emerged, and he whistled below his breath as he recognised Averil Dax.

Ellis's eyes softened as she rose and glanced at him across her shoulder. She was wearing a white knee-length dress which sparkled at the neckline and the diamond-shaped panel across her small waist. Her hair was swept up from its usual cut and fastened around the back of her head with a series of what Ellis had seen at once were genuine diamond clips. Her bare neck just begged for a diamond-drop pendant, and Ellis could almost imagine the exact carat, shape and colour for it. And how he'd order it to be cut.

The valet slipped into the driver's seat and roared off, and Ellis snapped out of his daydreaming. 'I've heard the Seahorse Grill is good,' he murmured, taking her arm.

Averil smiled. 'It is. Relax, you don't have to impress me, you know,' she said easily. Then added, so low that only Ellis could hear her, 'You've already done that.'

Ellis felt his heart skip a beat at her throaty, sexy, teasing voice, and grinned. Averil loved the way his amazingly green eyes flashed whenever he seemed to be in the grip of a strong emotion. Her own breath caught. Perhaps tonight was the night.

Outside, the valet parked the car in the hotel's security-conscious parking lot and then jogged to the nearest phone. The call he made was local, and didn't take him long. Tony Jackson paid very well to be kept informed of Averil Dax's movements, as every bellhop, waiter and parking valet on the islands knew only too well.

Inside, Ellis and Averil were seated at a discreet, candlelit table, semi-surrounded by screens sporting climbing vines. From the wine waiter he ordered Chambertin and Pouilly-Fuissé, and together they perused the menu. It was extensive, offering a range of cuisines, but they both plumped for local fare, starting with the fish chowder and following up with a wahoo salad for Averil and the grilled turbot for Ellis.

Averil smiled as she folded her menu away, rested her elbows demurely on the tabletop, folded her hands across one another, and rested her chin on them. Looking across the table at him, the candlelight reflecting in her dark, mysterious eyes, she smiled sexily. 'I can promise an equally grand choice of dessert for later,' she purred. She felt both silly and exhilarated, acting the vamp, and was instantly rewarded by another flash of peridot-green eyes.

'I'll expect something special then,' he purred back.

* * *

Tony Jackson was already dressed for a night on the town, but instead of making his way to the nightclub on St David's as he'd planned, he turned his scarlet sports car towards Paget. He wasn't really worried. He knew Averil occasionally dated other men, and although he didn't like it, he wasn't about to panic. He'd just take a quick look at his competition. Best not to let Averil see him though. She had a surprisingly annoying streak of independence which could flare up into a genuine temper whenever pressed.

In some ways, Tony liked this. He wanted a bit of fire and spirit in his chosen mate. In other ways, it made him want to slap her. Women who didn't know their place had to learn it.

* * *

Their plates were just being cleared away when Tony slipped onto a barstool and ordered a whisky. Through the open door he could see the restaurant, and lost no time finding Averil.

He caught his breath. She looked stunning. Absolutely stunning. And, for the first time, he felt the pangs of real fear hit him, because she'd never dressed up *quite* like that on any of their dates. He sipped his drink, which tasted unusually sour, and watched as they ordered dessert, wondering what all the laughter was about.

At their table, Ellis's eyes were practically glowing, like a cat's sighting a mouse in the grass. 'Is that all?' he murmured, affecting disappointment. 'Baba au rhum, compote of fruit, parfait and apricot snow. I thought you promised me a dessert to remember,' he shot across the table at her, making the waiter, who'd tensed up, suddenly relax and smile. He was not seriously decrying the chef's dessert tray after all!

'Well, I never said anything about *that* dessert being served here,' she demurred. Again, she felt silly but exhilarated. Flirting so outrageously was wonderful. She couldn't ever remember being allowed to be so outlandishly sexy before, and with a man who was doing it right back at her!

Both Ellis and the waiter caught their breath.

'I think we'll skip the food here,' Ellis said at once to the waiter, who shot an I-don't-blame-you-mate look right back at him. Averil couldn't help but giggle as the waiter melted discreetly away.

At the bar, Tony ordered a second drink, not liking the shining, glowing look on Averil Dax's face one little bit. He shifted on his seat to get a better look at the man with her, but all he could make out, since he was sitting with his back to Tony, was the expensive cut of his dark blue suit and the well-barbered blond hair. 'Hey, Franco, do you know the man dining with Miss Dax?' he asked, forcing himself to sound unconcerned, and the bartender, who'd been there since forever, obligingly looked and regretfully shook his head.

'No, sir. He's not staying at the hotel. Would you like me to ask around?'

Tony grunted, which Franco took for a yes.

At the table, Averil and Ellis rose, Ellis gesturing for the bill and tossing an American Express credit card onto the waiter's tray.

Tony was careful to turn around and face forwards as they passed through the door, but he needn't have bothered, he realised bitterly, as he shot them a look out of the corner of his eye. They had eyes only for each other.

Tony didn't like the feel of this. Not one bit. The glimpse that he'd had of his rival's profile revealed a youngish man, and whereas some men wore a good suit like an apology, this man, he'd seen at once, wore it as if he were doing it a favour. And Tony, who knew Savile Row tailoring when he saw it, tossed back his drink and slunk off the stool.

Outside, Ellis tucked his parking ticket into his pocket. 'A stroll on the beach?' he asked instead, looking up at the near-full moon. 'The stars are out.'

Averil nodded. 'Just let me take these off,' she said, making his pulse rocket, until he saw her bend down and slip off her white, high-heeled pumps. He grinned and tossed them to the parking valet, telling him to put them in his MG. Averil watched the beaming-faced youth shoot Ellis an envious look before jogging off, and wondered why she didn't feel angry at all this macho male-bonding stuff. And realised, quite simply, that it was because she trusted this man beside her. She trusted him not to take her for granted. Trusted him not to belittle her, either in word or deed. Trusted him in a way she'd never trusted anyone before – not even Morgan.

Elbow Beach was silvered with moonlight and like-minded lovers. A horse and carriage dropped off an obviously honeymooning couple, who hurried into the hotel, the looks on their faces speaking of their desire.

Averil smiled, and she was glad that he'd asked for this walk on the beach. Although before she'd been impatient for them to get back to his penthouse, she knew he'd been right to delay the pleasure a little while longer.

Ellis, sinking into the sand with every step he took, headed for the more compacted, damp sand at the sea's edge, and stood looking out across the ocean. The waves whispered their way towards them, then retreated, as if to tease.

'Have you ever worried about disappearing into the Triangle?' he asked her softly, making her look at him quickly. He turned his head to gaze down into her eyes. 'Because I feel like the Bermuda Triangle's got me, and I'm never going to make my way back home again.'

Averil laughed, but her heart was beating so hard she could hardly hear it. 'It's strange you should say that,' she whispered back. 'I never believed it existed before.'

She was standing so close to him he could smell her perfume. 'But you do now?' he whispered, slowly lowering his head.

'Oh yes,' Averil murmured, reaching up to loop her hand behind his head, her fingers spreading out over the nape of his neck as she pulled his head closer to her own. 'I do now,' she whispered.

The sudden heat that overwhelmed them took them both by surprise. With his lips on hers, Ellis felt himself ignite. The cooling sea breeze might not have existed. It might have been midday; the moon seemed to pack as much heat as the sun. He pulled her closer, moulding her curves to his harder frame.

Averil moaned beneath his lips, not in protest but in surrender. She felt her knee bend and slip between his legs. She could hear the slight slithering rasp of her dress as it moved against the material of his suit. His tongue met hers, introduced itself, conquered and was conquered in turn.

Her eyes closed, shutting out the splendour of the Bermudan night to go to an even more beautiful place.

Ellis didn't know where the gentle rush of the waves ended and the pulse of his own bloodstream began. They seemed to melt into one another, as, in turn, they joined with the woman in his arms. When, finally, their lips parted, she opened eyes, huge and dark, and looked up at him.

'I love you,' she said. As simple as that.

'I love you,' he said. As simple as that.

But then something flickered in his eyes. The world came back. The stolen diamonds. Tony Jackson. The reason he'd met her in the first place. It all returned and he couldn't stop it. Like Canute, he couldn't hold back the sea of reality.

Averil saw the flicker of his eyes and went cold. 'What is it?' she cried, her throat closing with fear.

Ellis shook his head. 'Nothing,' he lied. 'Nothing. Let's walk.'

And so they walked along the beach, hand in hand.

And yet far, far apart.

* * *

Morgan had named his split-level palatial residence near Clarence Cove 'Olympus', partly because of his tongue-in-cheek sense of humour, partly out of defiance.

Not that he felt like those ancient Greek gods, who lived on high and looked down on mere mortals. Mostly he'd done it to remind himself that, though he'd climbed to the top of the mountain, it was a long way down, and very easy to take a fall. At the time, he'd been thinking more in terms of financial catastrophe, of course. An event which had never happened, and now seemed never likely to. What he hadn't counted on when naming his residence after the mythical abode of the gods was that a man could fall in more ways than one – and a long way too.

That night, as he stood on one of the many terraces overlooking the sea, he was forced to laugh at his own folly. It was ironic. Here he was, king of the castle, and a dirty rascal, in the irresistible form of Isadora Van Harte, had toppled him without him even knowing it.

Until it was too late.

He moved from the moon-washed terrace into his study and slowly sat down in his black leather swivel chair. He was expecting a call that evening, and he was both dreading it and impatient for it. He had used a firm of private inquiry agents for many years now, mostly to check out potential high-flying executives that he was considering hiring, and sometimes to check out competitors who might be dangerous.

He'd never thought he would need to hire them to investigate something for his private life. But then, before Isadora, he'd never thought a lot of things.

Oh, he was no monk. In fact, he'd once been married. It was after he'd graduated from Harvard and had gone to work in the bank. Dorothea (never Dottie!) had been the ideal wife of a prospective banker. Vassar-educated, poised, lovely, extremely social and the daughter of a high-ranking executive in IBM, she was just what the family had hoped for. And for a while, everything Morgan had thought he wanted too. But then he'd begun to change, and Dorothea, of course, hadn't.

He began to find the bank boring and confining, while Dorothea awaited with pleasure his next promotion. He began to travel widely, while Dorothea, who'd seen it and done it, preferred to stay in Boston and climb the social ladder. When he made the decision to come to Bermuda and start up his own business from scratch, it didn't surprise him, or dismay him, that she decided to stay behind. Frankly, she thought him mad, and had said so. The divorce had been largely amicable and mercifully rapid, and Morgan had never held her to blame. After all, it was *he* who'd changed. *He* who'd reneged on their unspoken deal. He'd let her down, and she'd cut her losses.

There had been so little of the pain and recrimination or sense of failure that they were supposed to feel that each realised, almost at the same moment, that they'd never truly loved one another. It had been a relief to be free, and Morgan had emerged from the experience a much wiser man. So when Averil came to him, fleeing from the same lifestyle and family pressures which had led him into making such a mistake, it was not surprising he'd been so firmly on her side.

After Dorothea, of course, he'd been far more careful. Nevertheless, one or two of his affairs had been intense and passionate, but even those, he'd known even at the time, were not love. In fact, he'd just got to the cynical, almost inevitable stage of thinking that love didn't even exist when . . . wham!

He laughed, then froze as his phone rang. For a long moment he sat staring at it balefully, then slowly reached forward and answered it. 'Morgan Dax.'

'Mr Dax. This is Gerald Farley here. You called the office and left a message for me to get back to you?'

Farley, Grainger and Dobbs were one of the best firms of PIs on the East Coast, but their contacts were international. Gerald Farley himself undertook most of the work that took him from the States.

'Yes, Gerald. Thank you for calling back. Your office said you were out in the field?'

'That's right. I'm calling from London, in fact,' Gerald said, which explained the slight hollowness on the line.

'In that case, I won't keep you,' Morgan said quickly. 'And it couldn't be better. Your being in England I mean,' he added. As he leaned back in the chair he could suddenly see Isadora again – her face, framed by that breathtaking waterfall of black hair, her big dark blue eyes looking up into his. A shaft of pain, so unexpected that it had him sitting suddenly upright in his chair, lanced through him.

'Oh? You have something for me to do over here, huh?' The voice in his ear was so normal, so far removed from his isolated world, that Morgan blinked. And with an effort, pulled himself together.

'Yes. I want you to send me all you can,' he cleared his throat, which suddenly felt as dry as sand, 'on a Miss Isadora

Van Harte. Home town Bournemouth. She's in her mid-twenties, and was booked on the flight to Bermuda that went down.'

Even as he spoke he felt more pain tugging at his subconscious. A warning that he was going to pay for this particular piece of prudent treachery.

'A bad business that,' Gerald Farley said soberly. 'Wasn't she the only survivor?'

'Yes. She's currently living over here with her aunt.'

'OK. Is there, er, anything specific you want me to find out? Men friends?' the investigator asked delicately.

Morgan felt his hand clench the phone so tightly his fingers began to ache. With something of an effort he relaxed his grip. 'Men friends certainly,' Morgan forced himself to say calmly, rationally. 'But not exclusively. I want everything you can find on her from the moment she was born. I even want old copies of her school reports, if you can find them. Details of any employment, you name it.'

'Right. And photos?'

'Yes, anything,' Morgan said, wanting nothing more than to get off that phone. 'As soon as you can, Farley,' he said abruptly, and hung up.

In London, Gerald Farley was slightly surprised. It was not like Morgan Dax, one of his more high-flying regular clients, to be so high-handed. Although rich, Gerald hadn't pegged him as arrogant. But then, unless he missed his guess, this Isadora woman had Morgan tied up in knots. It happened even to the best of them. He shrugged. It was none of his business. He had just a few more things to clear up for his current client, perhaps taking a day or two, then he'd catch the train to Bournemouth. One thing was for sure – any little secret that she was trying to hide wouldn't stay secret for long. Gerald was one of the best.

Back in Bermuda, Morgan sat back, staring balefully at the phone. He felt low. As low as a man could get. No matter how much he tried to tell himself that he was justified in checking her out, he couldn't shake the feeling that he'd just betrayed her. Worse, he felt like a second-hand voyeur. And it felt bitter. 'Damn you, woman,' he said softly. 'Damn you.'

* * *

Outside, an MG pulled up to the gates, which were electronically operated. Averil peered out of the windscreen, to let the security guard who'd be watching the camera recognise her. A moment later the gates swung open. Ellis drove to the main entrance but didn't turn off the engine. That alone told Averil all she needed to know. She turned to him, telling herself that she was not, *not* disappointed. Insisting to herself that she was not afraid either.

'Well,' she said, trying to sound bright but only succeeding in sounding hollow. 'That was a wonderful evening.'

Ellis smiled grimly. 'Some of it was wonderful,' he corrected softly. He knew she'd expected him to take her to his place. To make love to her. But he just hadn't been able to. Not with so many secrets between them. He'd been tempted, oh so very tempted, to just confess everything to her, and trust to her forgiveness. He was almost sure she'd give it. Even with her hang-up about people using her.

But the thought of Tony Jackson stopped him. The man was dangerous. And she was close to him still. Who knew what might happen if she somehow got caught up in things?

'Ellis,' Averil murmured, an obvious question in her voice.

He sighed heavily and reached out to touch her cheek. 'I meant what I said on the beach,' he said softly.

'I know,' she said, her face suddenly lighting up. It was the only thing keeping her going. 'Is it another woman?'

She sounded so brave, Ellis felt like kicking himself. 'No, sweetheart. It's nothing like that. I swear.'

Averil nodded, believing him instantly. 'In that case, you'll have to come to dinner here one evening. Meet the dreaded family.' She tried to make a joke out of it. 'Well, Morgan at least. I think you'll like him. You're so very much alike.'

Ellis nodded. 'I'd like that,' he said. And meant it. Slowly he reached across the gear lever and kissed her. 'Call me?' he said.

Averil almost laughed out loud. 'Oh, you can rely on *that*,' she said firmly. Like her brother, she never backed down. She didn't know what the problem was yet, just that there was one. But she'd worm it out of him. And overcome it. Now that she'd found love at last, she wasn't about to let go of it without an almighty fight!

* * *

Tony Jackson was in bed when the call came. He answered it, staring fiercely up at the ceiling. 'Yes?' he snapped.

'Hi, Mr Jackson, it's me, Franco.'

The bartender. Tony had not forgotten he'd asked him to find out the identity of Averil's hot date. 'Yes, Franco. Did you find out anything?'

'Sure did, Mr Jackson. His name is Ellis Reynolds, and he's taken a three-month lease on one of those fancy condos over by Devonshire Dock.'

Tony shot upright, going as pale as he ever went. 'Reynolds? Is he English?'

'Yes, sir.'

Tony was quiet for so long that the bartender became restless. 'Is that all right, Mr Jackson?'

Tony gave himself a mental shake. 'Yeah, yeah, that's fine. You'll be getting a little bonus through the post,' he added vaguely, and hung up.

Reynolds wasn't an uncommon name, Tony knew. But how many men could there be in the world named *Ellis* Reynolds? And could it be a mere coincidence that the half-owner of Reynolds-Smythe just *happened* to show up in Bermuda? He didn't think so! Restlessly, his rat-like instincts warning him of trouble, Tony got up and poured himself a long, stiff drink. So the rumours he'd heard about Reynolds-Smythe not taking the diamond heist lying down were turning out to be true. And now that bastard Reynolds was here. On *his* island. Chasing after *his* girl. No doubt angling to get to him through her.

Tony swore and threw the glass with sudden violence at the wall. It shattered with a satisfying crash. One of his two goons rushed in, saw the glass, saw the glowering expression on his boss's face, and hastily backed out again.

Tony began to pace. How had Reynolds got on to him? He couldn't have traced the stolen stones themselves to Bermuda. Tony knew the courier, and he was a wily, paranoid son of a bitch. He'd never have allowed himself to be traced. Someone must have grassed.

Unless . . . Had Robbie Dacres contacted him? Perhaps the beach bum hadn't been so stupid after all. Having the stones was not the same as being able to fence them. Perhaps Dacres had meant to sell them back to Reynolds all along? Such an arrangement was hardly unheard of. Some thieves, he knew, made a habit of selling back their loot to the original owners.

But if so, did that mean that Ellis Reynolds knew where the stones had been hidden? Or at least had a good idea?

His first thought, to just kill Reynolds, slowly faded. He needed to think this through. And he needed to call Averil Dax. He smiled, a slow, hateful smile. Oh yes, he needed to speak to Averil Dax. Both to find out what she knew and to see if Mr Stick-his-nose-in-where-it-wasn't-wanted Ellis had told her who he was and what line of business he was in.

Somehow he thought not.

TEN

Chance pulled the big limousine to a halt outside the electronic gates at Olympus and gave a cheerful honk. It was not strictly necessary, for even as he sounded the horn the gate was opening. 'Hidden security cameras, dear,' Elizabeth whispered to Imogen in the back seat, as the English girl watched, fascinated. In her world, front doors were usually guarded by nothing more fearsome than the odd garden gnome!

'I see. Does he have bodyguards too?' she murmured, wondering if the two goons who'd been so anxious to speak to Imogen Dacres were on Morgan's payroll. She didn't think that the fact that Morgan *seemed* not to know them proved anything.

By now Chance had pulled up outside the main entrance and was opening the door for the ladies. 'I doubt it, dear,' Elizabeth replied, sounding amused as she climbed stiffly out. 'If ever a man was able to take care of himself it would be Morgan. He does karate. Or jujitsu, or one of those martial arts. Black belt too.'

Imogen smiled wryly. Terrific. Perhaps it was just as well she hadn't slapped his face the other day in the exotic house! She might have landed up on her back on the floor. A tight little ache of desire suddenly started throbbing deep down inside of her at the thought.

Ruthlessly she squashed it. Only to find the image of him towering over her, all slicked with sweat, popping into her mind like a cork from a bottle. Imogen bit her lip. This was going to be one hell of a long evening if she couldn't keep better control over her fantasies than this!

She hadn't been keen to come to dinner at Morgan's place at all, but Elizabeth wouldn't have dreamed of turning Averil's invitation down. 'I'm really looking forward to meeting this young man of Averil's,' Elizabeth confided, using her cane heavily as they walked towards the open door. 'It's the first time she's brought one home, so to speak. I think Morgan's curious too.'

Imogen let Elizabeth's words wash over her, for the man holding open the door wasn't a butler, as she'd half expected, but Morgan himself. He was dressed casually but well, in cool white slacks and a dark green silk shirt which complemented his dark blond hair to perfection. His collar and top two buttons were undone, revealing a column of bronzed skin. She wondered if opening a third button would reveal the same golden hairs on his chest as she could remember lightly coating his legs. And if they were long enough to run her fingers through them. Damn!

She dragged her racing breath into a more controlled rhythm and forced herself to smile noncommittally as she mounted the first of the two shallow fan-shaped steps. 'Morgan,' she said, far more calmly than she felt.

'Isadora,' he murmured, with just a hint of tit-for-tat mocking formality. And Imogen went visibly pale. It puzzled him, of course, because he had no way of knowing how much it hurt her to have him call her by another woman's name.

Just once, Imogen thought painfully, she'd like to hear her own name on his lips. And in the deep recesses of her treacherous mind she could hear him saying it. *Imogen. Imogen.* Calling her name hoarsely, the way he'd say it if they were in bed together . . . NO!

Imogen blinked and looked away, her face tight.

Puzzled, intrigued and annoyed (par for the course, he thought wryly), Morgan transferred his attention to Elizabeth. 'Elizabeth, you look charming as always,' he said urbanely.

Elizabeth smiled. 'I look all right,' she corrected. In jade-green trousers and a mandarin-style fitted jacket of jade, aquamarine and orange, she knew she looked stylish. 'It's Isadora who looks charming,' she emphasised.

Imogen flushed. She was wearing a black silk calf-length dress with a deep V neck and figure-hugging cut. Her black hair was piled atop her head in a mass of clever loops and whorls. At her ears, borrowed diamond earclips sparkled in the moonlight. They were her only jewellery.

'Oh, I had noticed,' Morgan said. In point of fact, she'd taken his breath away for a few moments. 'Come on in. Averil's mysterious guest hasn't arrived yet.'

Elizabeth smiled. 'Nervous?'

'She seems all right.'

'Not her,' Elizabeth tapped him playfully on the wrist as he helped her through the door. 'You.'

'Me? Why should I be nervous?' he raised one eyebrow imperiously, but his eyes were twinkling.

Imogen followed Elizabeth inside, and was overwhelmed with a mass of sensory information. The floor beneath her was marble – a lovely creamy green-veined marble that swirled around her like a sea of stone. The walls towered above her, at least up to two storeys, and were of a pale matching green. A twisted spiral staircase, so silver it gleamed, led to the upper floors. Splashes of greenery in pots were everywhere.

He led them through the hall and down another few steps onto a level overlooking the sea. Massive picture windows and French doors gave the impression that one side of the house was nothing but glass. White leather sofas and chairs littered a massive room, the floor of which was also marble, but black this time. The paintings which hung on the walls were vivid splashes of colour, and were mostly, she was surprised to note, by local artists, depicting local scenes.

'Drink?'

'Champagne, please,' Elizabeth said at once. 'The pink kind if you have it,' she added extravagantly.

'Pommery coming up,' Morgan promised, heading for a huge black-glass bar at the far end. 'Isadora?'

'Orange juice please,' she said automatically.

'Make that a Buck's fizz,' Elizabeth corrected, exasperated. 'I'm trying to teach this girl some bad habits. She's deplorably lacking in them, I've found.'

Everyone laughed, and at that moment, Averil entered. She was dressed in a sparkling red outfit of jacket over mini-skirt, which should have overwhelmed her fair colouring but somehow didn't. It was the bold brown eyes, Elizabeth thought approvingly, and smiled at her.

'You look ravishing, dear. Your young man won't be able to take his eyes off you.'

Averil laughed. 'That was the general idea. Isadora, glad to see you again. Thanks for coming.'

Imogen smiled in genuine response. She'd first met Averil Dax at her own party, and had instantly hit it off with the rich American. There was something so open and honest and unassuming about her which had put Imogen at ease. Since then, they'd met up for a window-shopping spree and a coffee, and had arranged to go hiking together next week.

'Thanks for inviting me,' she said warmly.

At that point, an intercom buzzed, and Morgan walked over to it. 'Mr Reynolds, sir,' a male voice, presumably from the booth near the gate, came over the intercom.

'Show him in,' Morgan said, glancing at his sister speculatively. She was already heading for the door, an eagerness in her step and a flash in her eye that he'd never seen before. Obviously his sister had fallen hard for this guy. He found himself hoping against hope that he liked him.

Imogen watched him return to the bar and fix the drinks, accepting her glass without meeting his eyes. If she did, who knew what image might pop into her damned head! Probably herself, reclining on a beach, dressed in the skimpiest of bikinis, while he poured the drink over her and licked it off slowly.

Elizabeth glanced curiously at her young companion as she heaved a massive sigh, and saw that she was scowling.

At the door, Averil watched the MG pull to a halt and Ellis climb out. He was dressed in black, but had taken her at her word and kept it semi-casual. Black denim jeans (but designer and elegant) hugged him tightly, while a plain black shirt showed off his very fair colouring to perfection. As he came nearer, she could see his eyes glowing like a cat's and she felt her breathing go all to pot.

She walked down the steps to meet him. 'Before we go in, I wanted to tell you something,' she said firmly. Ellis, sensing that she had something important to say, halted just in front of her. Instinctively he reached out for her hands and held them gently.

'The other night, after you dropped me off here, Tony Jackson called me,' she said quickly, wanting to get it out of the way and over with.

Ellis blanched. Luckily though, Averil was so intent on saying her piece that she didn't notice. 'He was a man I've had a few dates with in the past. I wanted you to know I officially ended it with him.'

Ellis swallowed with difficulty. 'I see.'

Averil looked at him anxiously, misunderstanding his curtness. 'We were never really an item,' she assured him. 'I mean, not intimate or anything. But I didn't feel comfortable, letting him go on thinking, well, that he could just call me up and invite me to the theatre anymore. You know what I mean?'

Ellis nodded, struggling to come to terms with what she was saying. 'I see. Thank you.' Damn it, how could he ask her if that was *all*. He could hardly demand to know what else Jackson had told her. As it turned out, he didn't need to.

Averil took a deep breath. 'He also told me that he'd heard I was seen around town with you.'

Ellis tensed. 'Did he now?'

Averil nodded. 'He wondered what a diamond merchant was doing in Bermuda. Hardly the diamond centre of the world, was how he put it.' There was a distinct question in her voice now. 'Why didn't you tell me you were in the diamond trade?' She was a little surprised and hurt that he hadn't been more forthcoming.

Ellis felt his nerve endings quivering. What the hell was Jackson up to? How had he got on to him? And why tell Averil?

'Ellis?' she prompted, a touch of fear in her voice now. He'd seemed so far away just then.

Ellis pulled himself together with a snap. 'I'm in Bermuda to take a holiday, not on business, so the fact that there are no stones to buy over here isn't important. And I didn't tell you specifically what I imported and exported because, like all diamond dealers, security and secrecy has become something of a habit with me.' He shrugged. 'Does it really matter?' he asked softly.

Averil smiled tremulously. 'No, of course it doesn't. It was just from the way Tony was going on, I felt it was some big deal, that's all.'

Ellis's smile became forced. 'How was he going on?'

Averil shrugged, a small puzzled frown creasing her golden brows together as she thought back. 'I'm not sure. It's hard to describe. It's like he was angling for something. But when I told him that I wouldn't be seeing him again, I could tell he was angry. I got the impression that he wanted to know if I knew – what you did for a living I mean,' she said, and laughed at her own confusion.

Ellis's smile was now so forced he felt his cheeks aching. Damn! Something had gone wrong. Tony Jackson was on to him. He'd have to be careful from now on. But at least Averil was out of it. She was surely safe enough, if only because of who she was: the sister of Morgan Dax, a man of enormous power and influence. Sewer rats like Tony were always careful never to tread on the big boys' toes. He forced himself to relax, and squeezed her hands. 'Forget about him. He's history. And if you want to know about the diamond business, I'll tell you all about it. Anything you like.'

Averil was nobody's fool. She knew there was something going on, but now, at least, she had it classified. It was something to do with business, and as such, not a personal threat. 'Well, it's certainly more glamorous than import-export, you must admit,' she laughed, taking his arm and leading him inside.

Everyone looked up as they walked into the room. They made a striking couple. Elizabeth was not the only one who had an immediate sense of 'rightness' about them.

Morgan walked forward, his eyes friendly but watchful. 'Morgan Dax,' he said, holding out his hand.

Ellis met the level gaze with an easy but equally watchful look. 'Ellis Reynolds,' he said, and the two men shook hands.

Imogen felt nervous for Averil – she knew how much she wanted these two men to hit it off. 'You two were so long out there I was thinking of sending out a search party,' Elizabeth's amused voice eased the moment, and Averil laughed.

'Sorry. Ellis, this is Elizabeth Van Harte, a kind of stand-in aunt of ours. And Isadora, Elizabeth's niece.'

Ellis came forward to take Elizabeth's hand. He made no attempt to kiss it, or anything continental or fancy. He simply shook her gnarled hand carefully, suspecting arthritis. 'Glad to meet you,' he said simply, but meant it. Averil had talked of Elizabeth often, and with real affection, and he was inclined to think anyone Averil liked was all right with him. He turned to Imogen, the strictly male part of him noting her beauty, but not coveting it. 'Isadora,' he said, and smiled.

Imogen found herself liking him. He was gorgeous, of course, but not as gorgeous as Morgan, and there was something about him which inspired confidence. 'Mr Reynolds.'

'Ellis.'

'Drink, Ellis?' Morgan asked briskly, not liking the picture of them together.

Ellis straightened easily and walked over to the bar, where Morgan waited. 'Mineral water would be great,' he said.

Morgan raised an eyebrow. 'Can't tempt you with anything stronger?'

Ellis smiled and shook his head. 'I'm driving.'

For a moment a long, almost telepathic look seemed to pass between them. Although it was early days, Morgan found himself relaxing as he poured the water. He glanced at Averil, two pairs of dark eyes meeting, and he smiled slowly.

Averil almost clapped. He liked him! She'd been sure he would, of course, but even so . . . She felt her tenseness melt away. After that, the evening progressed easily as the conversation and getting-to-know-you process began.

Ellis made no bones about his poor background, but he was neither apologetic nor belligerent about it, merely honest. As they walked into the dining room, one level down (Elizabeth and Imogen using the lift), the atmosphere had distinctly mellowed.

The first course was beluga caviar with chopped boiled eggs and raw onion, served with melba toast and wedges of lemon – something Imogen had never tried. It was salty.

'So, you spend most of your time in Antwerp and Amsterdam?' Morgan asked, looking across the table at Ellis.

'Right. My partner, Justin, spends more time in Israel.'

'Justin?' It was Averil who spoke.

Briefly, Ellis gave them a potted history of Reynolds-Smythe. 'So you see, Justin provides the image, represents the stability, and generally makes everyone feel like they can trust us, while I do the financial stuff and planning.'

Morgan, who'd easily read between the lines, nodded. Ellis was the brains, Justin the front. 'And you're happy with that?' he asked mildly. He was a little surprised – he'd had Ellis pegged as a one-boss kind of man, like himself.

Ellis glanced at him. 'Yes,' he said, equally mildly. 'A lot of partnerships don't work because of jealousy, which is usually caused by one partner wanting to encroach on the territory of the other. With Justin and me, that's never happened. Besides, it was his money that started us off. He needn't have gone in with me, and he was taking a chance in doing so.' Ellis shrugged. So the unspoken implication was that Justin had his loyalty.

Morgan nodded, understanding at once. It spoke well for the man's character, and any lingering doubts which he might have had slowly began to fade. Besides, one thing was obvious: Averil was head over heels in love with him. And that fact alone meant that Morgan was willing to give Ellis an awful lot of benefit of the doubt.

'So you never get back to your homeland much?' Elizabeth took up the gambit as the plates were cleared away by a pair of quietly efficient waiters.

'Oh, I wouldn't say that,' Ellis demurred. 'London has a thriving diamond centre.'

'But how does it all work?' Elizabeth asked, as lobster soufflé was put in front of them.

'Yes, I wondered that,' Averil said, smiling across at him adoringly.

Imogen felt her heart ache. Averil was so obviously in love with him, and there was nothing in the world to stop her from showing it. Whereas she hardly dared look at Morgan. She took a mouthful of the delicious-looking seafood concoction, actually tasting very little of it.

'Well, it's simplicity itself really,' Ellis began obligingly. 'Say you go to the Bursa in Israel. You know more or less what stones you want to buy. Uncut, cut, weight, colour, etc. You have, say, a jeweller who needs such and such. So you go into the trading centre with a "want list".'

The people around the table nodded, even Imogen began to be taken out of herself by the interesting topic. 'Sellers then come and check those lists to see if they have what you're interested in, and if they have a match, you haggle.'

Morgan grinned. 'Why do I get the impression it's not quite as simple as all that?' he challenged.

Ellis laughed. 'Well, you have to know what you're doing,' he admitted. And nobody at the table had any doubts at all that Ellis was a man who knew what he was doing.

As the main dish of beef Wellington was served, the conversation became more varied. Elizabeth regaled them with memories of a killer game of bridge, involving a visiting bishop (promptly made insolvent), a very famous movie star (who threw a wobbly, much to everyone's satisfaction), and a woman who'd been caught cheating with the aid of her highly trained pet Yorkie dog. According to Elizabeth, the pooch lurked beneath her mistress's chair and promptly sat on any card dropped to the floor after her mistress had palmed it.

The wine, Moet et Chandon and Soave, flowed freely, but Ellis kept to mineral water. As did, by and large, Imogen.

It was nearing midnight when, the dessert cleared away, and coffee and cheese and biscuits residing on the table for any takers, Imogen made a mistake. It had been an easy enough one to make, and she just hadn't seen it coming.

The conversation was on London. Averil, of course, had been there, as she'd been to most places at some time or other, but only as a visitor. Ellis, as a native, was telling her all about the things she'd never seen – Portobello Road, the meat and fish markets, Canary Wharf.

'Did you get to town much, dear?' Elizabeth asked Imogen mildly, who laughed and shook her head. 'Good grief no. No reason to.'

'You preferred your home town?' Elizabeth nodded. 'I can't say I blame you.'

Imogen smiled. 'If I lived here I wouldn't want to go anywhere else,' she said. 'Mind you, a lot of people say the same about Oxford. And it is such a lovely city.'

Averil smiled. 'Ah, the dreaming spires. I've never been there, but I must go one day.'

Morgan, who'd been reaching for a piece of gorgonzola, paused. Slowly his eyes lifted to hers. 'I thought you came from Bournemouth, Isadora?' he said softly.

Imogen felt herself shrivel inside, and cursed her stupidity. When would she learn to guard her tongue? The trouble was, it was such a strain having to be careful all the time.

And her nerves were still shredded by the dreadful aeroplane accident. 'Oh, yes, I do,' she answered hoarsely, reaching for the coffee pot and pouring out a cup, desperately trying to cover her tracks by giving herself something to do. 'But I visit Oxford whenever I can.'

'Oh?' Morgan asked, not fooled for one minute by her downcast eyes and busy hands. He scented blood. 'Why?'

Elizabeth came to her rescue. 'Oh, Morgan, don't be so dense! Why, if I lived in England, I'd spend all my time visiting the lovelier cities too. Oxford and Bath and York and . . . what's that other place? The one with the cathedral?'

Imogen could have kissed her. 'Which one? Salisbury? Ely? Canterbury?'

'Canterbury!' Elizabeth confirmed, noting the panic in Imogen's eyes. 'You know,' she yawned very delicately behind her hand, 'I don't want to be a party-pooper but I'm feeling rather tired.'

Instantly Imogen and Averil got to their feet. 'Oh, Elizabeth, of course. We've kept you up so long,' Averil began.

'I'll call Chance,' Imogen said at the same time. And so, in the general fuss, Imogen got away with it.

But as his guests were driven away in their limousine for the short journey home, Morgan's mind was working furiously. Isadora had spoken of Oxford as if it was somewhere she lived, not merely visited. And Elizabeth had very conveniently helped her gloss it over. What the hell was going on? He was so engrossed in the mystery that when Averil kissed him goodnight and got into the MG with Ellis he barely noticed. Not that he'd have said anything if he had – he was not her keeper, and she was long past the age when she could spend the night elsewhere whenever she wanted to.

But she'd never done so before, and it was to be some hours later before he noted the fact. Even then, it didn't worry him. Ellis Reynolds had passed the meeting-the-family test with flying colours.

* * *

Averil walked a little nervously around the penthouse, then slipped off her shoes as Ellis poured them a nightcap of brandy in huge bulbous glasses. Outside, the sea breezes blew in from the tropical night, bringing the scent of frangipani. Slowly they came together and clinked glasses. Ellis's eyes, by now, would have made even a cat green with envy!

'You're beautiful,' he said softly.

'So are you,' Averil replied promptly.

Slowly, he reached out and took the glass from her, setting it on the low occasional table nearby. She came into his arms as naturally as he breathed. Their lips met and held as he slowly pushed the jacket from her shoulders and let it slither to the floor. The sound of her mini-skirt zip being undone made her smile beneath his lips, before that too was on the floor. Now her own hands fumbled for his jeans, and this time it was his turn to smile as the sound of an unfastening zip once again sounded in the silent room.

Her hands moved up to his shirt, unbuttoning. His own hands moved between her shoulder blades to unclip her bra. And still their lips clung together.

He reached around, cupping her tender breasts, his thumbs rubbing her nipples, and she gasped, finally breaking the kiss. He opened his eyes to look down into her face, her eyes enormous dark pools in her face. 'Ellis,' she whispered.

Without a word, he picked her up and carried her to the big four-poster bed, pushing aside the gauzy netting. He stood, briefly, to struggle out of the tight-fitting jeans, made all the more difficult because of his arousal.

Averil giggled.

But then he was crawling up the bed towards her, the moonlight silvering his hair and picking out the moving, rippling muscles on his body as he did so, and all giggling abruptly stopped. He pulled down her panties, tossing them over his shoulder, his hands caressing her ankles before he pulled her legs gently apart.

Averil's eyes feathered closed as he kissed the inside of first one ankle then the other. The tender skin in the dent of first one knee then the other. Her heart pounded as he trailed hot kisses up her thighs. Her back arched as he found her centre, the very feminine core of her, and his tongue flickered hot traceries, sucking and nibbling until she was writhing on the bed, and his hands spanned her waist, forcing her still as he drove her sweetly insane. She cried out, shuddering, then gasped as he slid fully atop her, entering her just as her first orgasm pulsed and setting off another one.

Ellis, his jaw clenched tight, his eyes slumberous, loved the way her pretty face contorted with passion. He channelled his physical power ruthlessly, feeling muscles and tendons and sinews obey his commands. Slowly, with infinite patience and rhythm, he had her writhing and screaming, again and again, determined to make this a night to remember.

Somewhere, in the deep dark hours of the night, his own control fled, and he moaned her name into the night, collapsing atop her, feeling her arms come around him, her hands stroking him, her soft voice uttering his name over and over and over again.

He slept, with the tip of her nipple making an indentation in his cheek which would make them laugh in the morning, sharing a moment strictly reserved for lovers.

ELEVEN

Morgan tied the rope around Imogen's waist, his lips twisting wryly as he did so. At last he'd tied her to him. At least for the next hour or so anyway!

Imogen watched him a shade anxiously as he put on a pair of goggles and checked his tanks. She still wasn't quite sure just how she came to be on his boat, the *Manta*, a mile from Daniel Island, and dressed in full diving kit.

Oh, the sequence of events was clear enough. She and Elizabeth had been sitting around the pool yesterday, Imogen trying to think of a way to get access to Robbie's autopsy reports, when Morgan had just 'dropped by'.

The fact that he had had an ulterior motive didn't become immediately clear until he mentioned to Elizabeth that Imogen had been enquiring about diving at his school. At first Imogen had tensed up, thinking he was fishing for information, but instead she found herself being very expertly manoeuvred into taking diving lessons with him.

Elizabeth had been entranced by the idea, telling her that she would enjoy the experience enormously. And with Morgan, she'd be in very safe hands. After that, it had been all but impossible for Imogen to refuse his offer of tuition, and, surprise, surprise, he happened to have all the equipment they'd need in his jeep.

So, bewildered, but with a growing sense of excitement, she allowed herself to be fitted out and given a 'preliminary' right there in Elizabeth's pool.

Imogen hadn't put up much of a fight, truth be told. Since Robbie had died in a supposed diving 'accident' she could hardly complain now that she was being handed on a golden platter the opportunity to learn all about diving.

Of course, she could only expect to learn the mere basics, even after three hours of intensive practice in the pool. Even so, she quickly picked up a lot of helpful information.

When Morgan had finally left, well pleased with her progress, they'd agreed to meet the next day to go on her first sea-dive. Now though, as the boat gently rocked beneath her and she looked around at the vastness of the ocean, she wasn't so sure. Just beyond was Daniel's Head on Somerset Island, but although it looked close she wasn't deceived. Still, the ocean was like a millpond and the sun was shining. The boat's pilot, 'Skinny', was obviously very well qualified, and knowing that he was to remain up here, checking that everything was all right, gave her some much-needed reassurance.

And now there was the rope being tied around her waist, securing her to Morgan. She was even more thankful for that. The ocean looked very big, and she was beginning to feel very small.

Morgan, dressed in a black wetsuit with yellow stripes, sat on the side and put on his flippers, watching her closely. He'd helped her on with her gear, wondering how much she remembered from yesterday. He wouldn't dream of telling her, of course, but he suspected that she was a natural. 'All right?' he asked softly.

Imogen took a deep breath and walked the length of the rope's twenty feet to join him. She reached down for her own flippers. 'I think so,' she said honestly.

She knew they'd gone through everything she needed to know yesterday. They'd gone through it and gone through it and gone through it until it felt drummed into her head forever. First, he'd explained the equipment to her – what it did, how it worked and what she must look out for. The very simplest things were self-evident. The face mask, for instance. But even that, she'd learned, needed to be used properly. Although it allowed for perfect visibility underwater, he'd told her it had the effect of making everything look larger, a fact that hadn't been so obvious in a swimming pool. If too tight, he warned her, it would give her a headache, but he'd instinctively chosen just the right size for her.

Now she checked the recesses of it on either side of her nose which allowed her to pinch her nose from the outside, allowing her to clear her ears, which was, she now knew, essential. She also nervously checked the purge valves, which ensured she could expel air from the mask without removing it, and thus avoid breaking the seal.

He watched her approvingly.

She was dressed in a bright red diving suit, the better for him to be able to visually pinpoint her, although on this first, shallow dive, and being roped together, it was less important than it might have been. She put on her fins, making sure they weren't too loose, which might cause chafing; another hazard he'd warned her of yesterday. As she'd changed into the rubber suit only ten minutes ago, the first shiver-making coolness of it had rubbed off and now she was beginning to feel uncomfortably warm.

'Let's just go through the hand signals again,' he said, his dark eyes watching her from behind the mask. Instantly, she obeyed.

'OK?' he asked. And she made an O signal.

'Something's wrong.' And she held her palm out flat and level, but her thumb going down and up.

'Distress,' he said sharply, and she clenched her fist and waved it from side to side.

'Go down or I'm going down.' With her fist still clenched, she pointed her thumb down.

'And up?' She smiled and turned her thumb up.

He smiled and nodded. 'OK. You remember what I told you about pressure?' She nodded, looking a little anxious. 'Don't worry,' he said quickly. 'That's not going to apply here. Just remember, at a depth of thirty-three feet the pressure is doubled to two bars, at sixty-six feet it's three bars and so on. But we won't be going down anything like that far today. But if we did, what would I need to check was working all right first?'

'The aqualung's regulator,' she said promptly.

'OK. Run through the equipment on my suit with me. This?'

And so they went through it all again – the demand valves, regulators, compressors and cylinders, pillar valves, reserve valves, pressure gauge, weight belt and its various accessories, depth gauge, diver's compass and watch.

'You checked your own equipment?' he demanded.

'Yes.'

'Tanks?'

'Yes.'

'Good. Then we can go. You remember the rolling dive I taught you?' he asked.

Imogen grimaced and nodded. She hadn't been very comfortable with just rolling backwards into the pool, and to begin with had been about as graceful at it as a giraffe on roller skates. But now, as she adjusted her mask for the final time and checked her air, being careful not to bite down on the rubber in her mouth (a common mistake, Morgan had told her), she watched him roll backwards into the water, and mindful of the rope linking them together, quickly followed suit with barely a moment's hesitation.

And promptly learned that diving in a pool was *nothing* compared with diving in the ocean! To begin with, the sense of freedom was astounding. She almost felt as if she was floating in space, so vast did everything seem. She righted herself, using the fins a little awkwardly at first. Looking around, she instantly saw his black-suited body, comfortingly close, and gave him the OK sign.

The water temperature in winter, he'd told her, was in the high sixties, but it rose to the mid-eighties come the summer. Right now, though, she was glad of the cooling effect of it. Slowly he swam off ahead and she followed.

It was shallow here, she could see, which meant the light was fantastic. The bottom of the sea, she was a little surprised to realise (although she couldn't have said why), was as sandy as the beaches. Perhaps she'd expected rock?

As Morgan swam just above the sand, he suddenly stopped, waited for her to catch up and pointed downwards. She looked but could see nothing but sand. Then he waved his hand just in front of her, and a flat fish, half-buried in the sand, shot out of cover and swam off fast, making her jump.

Her bubbles intensified as she laughed, and quickly she stopped. Gave him the OK sign. And slowly they moved off again.

In the distance she could see a raised barrier of rock, which, as they got closer, transformed itself into multi-coloured corals and anemones.

She could understand why Robbie was so hooked on this sport. What a wonderful life, doing this for a living!

She stopped, making the rope tighten and causing him to look back at her, but she wasn't in trouble. Only entranced by a blue angelfish, swimming past her and making for the reef.

As he watched her, understanding how rapt she must be feeling, Morgan felt an incredible tenderness engulf him. He was glad he'd introduced her to this part of his world, and even more happy that she seemed to be taking to it so well.

As she began to follow him once more he had a sudden vision of the years to come: Isadora becoming as experienced a diver as himself. Afternoons spent exploring the more famous wrecks – the *Marie Celestia* or the *Darlington* – and then going home for cocktails on the terrace and reading the kids a bedtime story.

Whoa, he thought suddenly. Where the hell had that come from?

Imogen, totally unaware of his thoughts, was watching a red hind resting on the white sand below her. She wondered if they might see any turtles – either the green or loggerhead which Morgan had told her inhabited the waters here – but knew she mustn't be greedy. One thing was for certain though: diving was going to become a big part of her life.

Oh yeah? In Oxford? a sneering little voice piped up at the back of her mind, and instantly she felt depressed. Shaking it off, she told herself firmly to just enjoy it while she was here. And it wasn't hard to do. The fleeting, brightly coloured shoals of tropical fish were amazing – she'd only ever seen them in small tanks in aquariums before. Here they were as common as sparrows were in her own back garden.

As they got closer, she began to pick out the various corals. After Morgan had left the house, she'd got a book on marine life, and now had no trouble at all picking out some of the known species of rock coral, as well as the 'soft' corals like sea fans and sea rods.

She saw Morgan's hand waving, catching her attention, and she looked to where he was pointing and saw an impressive fish which, when they emerged later, he told her was a yellowtail rockfish.

Time simply flew, and when he tapped his watch, reminding her of their pre-set diving time limit, she was amazed. Could this have been what had caught Robbie out? This amazing acceleration of time? But no, she realised at once. Robbie was no novice. He'd had years of learning how to gauge time underwater.

She sighed but gave Morgan the signal that she understood, and slowly, reluctantly, followed him back to the boat. As if in consolation, however, they did see an even more impressive fish – the tiger rockfish – on their journey back.

As they broke the surface of the water, Skinny reaching down to give her a helping hand up, she was beaming. 'That was amazing,' she said when, mask and gear removed, she sat on the deck in the sunshine, feeling as if she'd just come back from another world.

They spent the return journey to Hamilton Harbour drinking fruit punch and planning their next dive.

Once back at Hamilton, Imogen didn't want to go, and Morgan didn't want her to leave, but she forced herself to walk up the jetty. He watched her, wondering ruefully what had happened to his plan to grill her more closely about the slip she'd made at dinner the other day.

* * *

Imogen wasn't the only one in downtown Hamilton that lunchtime. As she found a café with pretty wrought iron tables on the sidewalk, complete with gaily patterned parasols to shade her from the sun, Tony Jackson sat in the back of a black saloon car and watched a fair-haired man from behind darkened glass. He'd left the Maserati behind, as the anonymous saloon was far more fitting for what he had in mind. He glanced across the road at the bright yellow Mazda he'd bought on the sly two days ago. Inside it were two men Imogen would have recognised instantly, and Tony cursed them mildly. The fools had both windows wide open, their elbows hanging out, as large as life for anyone to see.

Why was he always surrounded by imbeciles?

Ellis walked with a loose-limbed gait along the esplanade, thinking cheerfully about diamond rings. He was certainly in the right business to know about them, and he was imagining the kind of stone he wanted to take to his master cutter.

A blue stone, he thought. And a large carat. Nothing but the best for Averil. As to the cut, 'brilliant' was still the best as far as he was concerned.

He stepped off the kerb and into the road, crossing it after looking carefully both ways. He'd been on the island long enough to be wary of the ubiquitous scooters and bicycles which could have you over as quick as winking. Of course, with the 20 mph speed limit strictly enforced, you always had plenty of time to leap back, yell, and choose your swear words!

He didn't see the black saloon car. Didn't know that inside it, Tony Jackson turned on the engine and crept slowly forward, the better to watch him and keep him in sight, checking to see that his idiot employees in the yellow Mazda were doing exactly the same.

Tony had had second thoughts about letting Ellis Reynolds live. After he'd been given the elbow by Averil, his anger had been slowly building and had now reached the point where Ellis was a walking insult. Besides, if Reynolds had known where the stones were, he'd have recovered them by now and been on his way.

But mostly Tony despised the blond-haired Englishman because, in a matter of days, he'd done something that Tony hadn't been able to do in months: win Averil Dax.

Now he smiled wolfishly, imagining her grief at the tragic loss of her lover. He could just see himself comforting her at the funeral. She would need a friend to turn to then, would she not? And who knew where that might lead?

Averil was too perfect a gem to pass up easily. All he needed now was a lull in the traffic and for his two idiot employees to get it right. He didn't need to be there himself, of course, but this was one contract he wanted to see fulfilled personally.

The Mazda owner, when questioned by police, would only dare say that he'd sold the car to a 'Mr Ford'. His description would be hazy. It would certainly never be traced back to Tony Jackson, society gadfly and wealthy supporter of charities. So long as nobody identified his two 'bodyguards' as the driver and passenger of the car that killed Reynolds, it would be a perfectly clean hit. Damn them, why didn't they roll up the windows? He knew it was hot, but even so . . .

Imogen was ordering her second cup of iced coffee when she saw Ellis. The café, on the corner of the main road and a little side street, had tables spilling right across the sidewalk, and he was stepping off the kerb to go around them. She was just starting to rise, to call to him, to smile, when she heard a car engine start up. There was something odd about it that for a moment she couldn't quite place. And then she understood. On an island where the top speed rate was twenty miles an hour there was no point revving the engine! But this one, she could hear, pulsated. As if the driver kept putting his foot down on the pedals. She turned, trying to pinpoint it, and among the line of parked cars a yellow one stood out – as did the smoke from its exhaust.

She turned back to Ellis, and saw him only yards away now, but with his profile to her. He obviously hadn't seen her, and was looking at the other side of the road, about to cross it.

The yellow car pulled slowly out of the line of traffic. As she watched, it stopped, facing forward. Ready to . . . what? Why wasn't it going?

Suddenly something cold yet also boiling hot filled her lungs, making her body ache. An instinctive, physical sense of doom. Quickly, she stepped around the table and began to move – no, *run* – towards Ellis.

She didn't even know why at that point.

Behind her, the waiter returned with her coffee and cried out in alarm, thinking that his beautiful customer was running out without paying her bill.

Several things then happened at once.

Ellis, who'd seen it was all clear and had stepped several feet out into the road, heard the dismayed shout of the waiter and turned his head their way. The man driving the yellow Mazda revved the accelerator as hard as he could and squealed towards Ellis, rapidly gaining speed. Imogen looked around and instantly recognised the two goons in the car. She turned back to Ellis. She was now running full pelt.

Ellis, distracted by the sight of a running woman, and one, moreover, that he suddenly recognised, stopped dead.

In his car, watching, Tony Jackson grinned widely. He said 'yes' softly to himself, and clenched his fist in victory. It couldn't be better. No way could they miss him now.

Imogen screamed, 'Ellis, look out!'

Ellis, reacting more to her horror than anything else, turned and took a puzzled step towards her. Out of his peripheral vision, he sensed something enormous, fast and yellow bearing down on him.

But now Imogen was there, and without conscious thought, simply flung herself into his side, literally catapulting both of them sideways over the bonnet of the car parked nearest to them. Ellis yelled as he banged painfully into the bonnet. The Mazda, swerving closer to the side of the road in order to hit him, found itself careening instead into the parked car.

As Imogen felt herself collide with Ellis, she also heard the sickening sound of rending metal. It was like the plane crash all over again! A primitive, atavistic fear washed over her as she and Ellis rolled in a tangle of limbs over the car and landed heavily and painfully onto the pavement beyond.

The Mazda lurched wildly, then shot off around the corner.

The waiter, who'd seen it all, stared, open-mouthed. Then he rushed to help Imogen up, berating bad drivers and swearing that they must have been tourists, not locals. He offered her a drink of brandy on the house – she was so pale, and shaking! Was she all right?

Ellis got quickly to his feet too, ignoring his own scrapes and bruises. 'Isadora,' he said bluntly. 'What the hell's going on?'

But Imogen was, for the moment, in no fit state to say anything. She was indeed shaking like a leaf.

Quickly, Ellis took her arm, and with the contrite waiter on her other side, they led her back to the table. There had been surprisingly few people on the street to witness the accident, which had happened so fast, and when even these few saw that nobody had been hurt they quickly lost interest. Besides, nobody wanted to have to hang around and give statements to the police. No doubt the owner of the now badly dented parked car had insurance.

'Here, sit down. Bring that brandy,' Ellis added to the waiter, who nodded and hurried off. When it came, Ellis held it to her lips and made her drink. The waiter left to return to his duties, but Ellis said nothing, merely waiting.

After a little while, some colour came back to her chalk-white cheeks. 'You were thinking of the plane crash, weren't you?' he said, gently matter of fact.

Imogen nodded. 'It brought it all back.'

'Yes,' he said grimly. 'I'm sure it did.' Only now did he begin to realise how close he'd come to death. 'The bloody maniac. What did he think he was doing? I guess he was probably drunk.' He sighed. 'You know, I probably owe you my life. That flying tackle you did,' he smiled, trying to make her laugh, 'it was like being in a James Bond movie.'

Imogen began to giggle, then couldn't stop. He watched her soberly, and without comment, as she struggled to bring herself under control. When she finally did so, she felt drained and utterly exhausted. Slowly, she lifted her eyes to his, and he saw the last of the shock fade away and something else take its place in her big blue eyes. Puzzlement, mostly.

'What?' he asked softly.

Imogen blinked, slowly coming to terms with the significance of what had just happened.

'Ellis,' she said quietly. 'That wasn't an accident back there.'

Ellis's eyebrows rose slightly. 'No? It certainly felt like one to me.' He rubbed his elbow ruefully. 'And I have the bruises to prove it.' He thought she must still be in shock after all, but her next words stopped him cold.

'No. I mean it was deliberate. The reason I got to you in time was because I recognised the drivers. I heard the car revving up. I saw it align itself on you, and I just *knew* what it was going to do.'

For a second, on that sunny sidewalk in the bright Bermudan sun, Imogen and Ellis stared at one another, chilled and now irrevocably linked. Then Ellis slowly let out a long, deep breath. 'I think,' he said quietly, 'you'd better tell me what's going on.'

Imogen, of course, had no real reason to tell him her secret. But she was tired of keeping up the pretence, and knew it would be such a relief to confide in someone at last – especially someone who now owed her, and would therefore keep it quiet. So she found herself doing just that – starting with who she really was. The strange letter from her brother. His so-called 'diving accident'. Her flight out here. The crash. The misunderstanding over her identity – and then the visit by the two goons driving the Mazda, demanding to know if the survivor was Imogen Dacres.

'So when I saw them again, driving the car, and you, in the road, I just knew your life was in danger,' she finished tiredly. She'd been barely speaking above a whisper, but he'd heard every word she said. And so much of it made sense.

Imogen looked at Ellis with the obvious question in her eyes, and he knew she was waiting for an explanation. And after she'd just saved his life and been so honest herself, he didn't hesitate.

When he'd finished, she was sat back in her seat, gazing at him hopelessly. 'You think this Tony Jackson has your diamonds then? And that Robbie was in on it?'

She didn't enjoy the thought of her brother's involvement, but she wasn't altogether surprised by it.

Ellis sighed. 'It looks like it. But . . .' he shook his head, frowning.

Imogen leaned forward eagerly. 'What?'

'Why was Robbie killed?' he asked simply.

Imogen looked back at him helplessly. 'I suppose he knew too much? Or,' hope flared briefly in her eyes, 'he didn't know what Tony Jackson was up to, and when he found out he threatened to go to the police and Jackson had him killed . . .' Her voice faltered. It just didn't sound like Robbie. Besides, she suddenly remembered what the bartender at the Beach Hut had said about Robbie boasting of his new-found wealth. Briefly, she told Ellis about it.

In the space of an hour they'd become joined by a common bond: Ellis to recover his diamonds, Imogen to find justice for her brother. Of course, Ellis nearly dying and her saving him cemented things even further. They were partners now.

'It does sound as if he expected a cut,' Ellis admitted. 'I'm sorry, I know he was your brother but that's what it sounds like to me.'

Imogen sighed. 'I know. But why would someone like Tony Jackson have to cut him in at all?' she asked.

Ellis nodded. 'It doesn't sound likely, does it?' he agreed. 'I think there's more to this than we know.'

'I agree.' She reached for her brandy and took another sip, still shivering.

Along the road, a Jaguar cruised slowly towards them. Morgan, on his way back from lunch with Averil, was going to drop her off at Elizabeth's before going on to his office. It was Ellis's fair head that Averil saw first. 'Look, there's . . .' she said brightly, then, her voice faltering, 'Ellis,' she finished faintly.

For she recognised the woman with him at the same time as Morgan did. And the fact that they looked so intimate, leaning over the table, heads close together. Even in the car, from a distance, they could both sense a kind of intensity about them. Their body language was fairly screaming closeness.

Morgan's hands tightened on the steering wheel.

'You're still in shock,' Ellis said to Imogen contritely, at that moment reaching across to take her brandy glass from her before she dropped it. He was shocked to find her hands so icy cold. 'Do you need a doctor?'

His hands closed over her cold fingers, feeling a profound sympathy for her. She'd been through so much. And he was only adding to her woes. To learn something bad about your brother was hard. But when that brother was dead . . .

In the car, Morgan and Averil saw them holding hands. And as they passed, they saw Imogen's face, absolutely radiant, looking across at Ellis. Averil felt a tight, hard pain squeeze her heart. Morgan felt murderous.

'Oh, Ellis, I've suddenly realised,' Imogen breathed. 'Those two men. Those goons. They work for Jackson!' she breathed.

Ellis looked surprised. 'Of course they do. Who did you think they worked for?' he asked, puzzled.

Imogen laughed. She was so incredibly happy. Morgan was innocent.

On the road, the Jaguar passed them slowly. Neither noticed.

'I thought . . . never mind,' Imogen said. 'But everything's all right now! Everything's wonderful in fact.'

Ellis shook his head. She was still obviously shaken by the near miss. She wasn't making much sense.

In the Jaguar, Morgan turned a tight, angry face towards his sister. Averil was pale and quickly turned her face away, hiding the shattered look in her eyes. 'It probably meant nothing,' he rasped.

But neither of them could quite make themselves believe it.

TWELVE

Morgan walked down the silver spiral staircase, glancing out onto the terrace as he did so. Averil, sitting in one of the wrought iron chairs, was gazing out at the sea, a cup of untouched coffee in front of her, now cold. He joined her, and a few moments later, Molly, their resident housekeeper, brought out a fresh pot. Morgan smiled as she left the tray, but made no move towards it.

'Did you sleep?' he asked his sister quietly, and she swung her level brown-eyed gaze from the ocean to her brother and smiled ruefully. She held a hand out in the air and turned it from side to side.

'So so. And you?'

Morgan lifted an eyebrow. 'Me? Why should I have lost any sleep over it?'

Averil smiled. 'Do remember who you're talking to,' she admonished softly. 'I've seen the way you look at Isadora.'

Morgan scowled. Averil gave him a semi-amused smile. 'If you want my advice, it's pointless to fight it,' she said. But there was not so much defeat as acceptance in her voice.

Morgan shot her a quick, worried look. 'Are you going to see him again?'

'Of course,' she said, stunned that he could ask. 'I love him.'

Morgan sighed. 'Right.'

'Besides, we don't know yet what that little tête-à-tête was all about,' she insisted stubbornly. 'And until I ask Ellis about it, and listen to his side of the story, I'm not going to jump to conclusions.'

'That sounds sensible,' Morgan said mildly, and Averil only just managed to curb the impulse to throw the coffee pot at him. She didn't *feel* like being sensible! She wanted to rant and rave and kick Ellis where it hurt, and then slap Isadora's beautiful face for her, and go to her room and cry herself sick. She laughed.

Morgan looked across at her and grinned. 'Hell, sis, we're a pair, aren't we?'

Averil agreed, and Morgan rose to pour some coffee at last. He took it to the terrace wall, which was waist-high and festooned with growing vines, and stared out across the ocean. The sea breeze ruffled his dark blond hair.

He felt utterly baffled. Nothing in his life had quite prepared him for this. He didn't know what to do. Go charging around to Elizabeth's and demand to know what the hell Isadora thought she was doing, playing fast and loose with his sister's boyfriend? Oh yeah, very mature that sounded.

Ignore it? Right, and let it go on eating away at him, like it had all last night and still was now?

Take Ellis to one side and . . . what? Persuade him to give up Isadora and concentrate on Averil instead? His lips twisted grimly. How the hell could he do that and still keep any shred of dignity or self-respect? Besides, Ellis was not a man who'd take kindly to interference in his private life.

And that was something else that puzzled him. From the way Ellis had looked at Averil at dinner the other night, he would have bet half his fortune that the man was genuinely smitten with her. And he hadn't seemed to take undue notice of Isadora when they'd first met. Oh, Morgan had seen the flash of interest, but with a woman as spectacular as Isadora, any one would feel the same. But it hadn't seemed anything *more* than that. And when had they arranged to meet for tea and cakes at the little café?

'You know,' he said out loud, 'it doesn't make sense.'

Averil, staring morosely into her coffee cup, looked up. 'What do you mean?'

'Ellis and Isadora. It doesn't add up. I would have known if they had been . . . if there had been a spark between them.' He turned around, leaning against the wall, looking at his sister. 'I've got sensitive radar as far as that woman is concerned,' he explained, somewhat bitterly. 'And if she'd been struck by Ellis I'd have known about it.'

Averil blinked, and slowly straightened up. 'You know, you're right. Ellis and I . . .' She thought back to that wonderful night of lovemaking. 'He wouldn't cheat on me,' she said, the thought coming out of nowhere but having undeniable substance. She began to smile, dazzlingly, as she repeated it slowly, savouring the words, 'He wouldn't cheat on me.'

Morgan hoped she was right.

When he left for the office half an hour later, Averil was in a much better mood, and he wondered if she'd be calling Ellis to have it out with him. He'd feel a lot better himself for hearing Ellis's explanation!

His offices occupied the top floor of a three-storey building, overlooking landscaped grounds in a semi-residential area of the city. He walked first into the outer office, checking for messages with his secretary, then went to his private rooms, opening all the windows wide. Outside, a palm tree made gentle rustling sounds as the wind blew through it. He was wearing his usual office ensemble – shorts and a loose fitting, short-sleeved shirt, his bare feet encased in sandals.

He went rapidly through the emails which needed his attention, and was nearly through when one in particular caught his attention. It was from Gerald Farley. The man certainly worked quickly.

Rapidly, Morgan opened the attachment and read Farley's report. It was all there – a complete biography of Isadora Van Harte. Her father had died relatively young, her mother only recently. Her school records weren't anything to write home about, but he wasn't interested in her academic prowess. He slowed as he read the report on her first boyfriend, then a long-term relationship with a man called Mark Brentwood, which ended when he left her for another woman.

The man must be mad, he thought grimly, fighting back the image of Isadora living with another man. Cooking him dinner. Washing his clothes. Walking hand in hand with him.

With a grunt, he quickly turned to the financial section. As he'd thought, the Van Harte family hadn't cut off their wayward son penniless. There'd been enough money to educate Isadora at Cheltenham Ladies' College, and from Farley's description of their five-bedroom home in an exclusive area of the seaside resort, they hadn't exactly had to worry about where the next meal was coming from. And yet, on the death of her mother, Isadora hadn't been exactly rolling in money. Over the years, their income had dwindled remorselessly.

With a sigh he turned to the pictures and froze.

The first one was a college picture, featuring rows of similarly dressed young women between sixteen and eighteen, one of them ringed. He stared down at the face, puzzled. True, it was a bad photograph – small and a little blurred – but that wasn't Isadora! Quickly Morgan turned to the others. A shot taken at a party – again, the woman ringed bore no resemblance to Isadora. She had lots of dark hair, yes, but that was the only similarity. Confused, and with a growing sense of unease, he turned to the next photograph. And there was no doubt now. It was a copy of Isadora Van Harte's driving licence. Morgan stared at the typewritten name. Isadora P. Van Harte. Then the signature. Then the photograph. The small square photo was full-faced and quite clear.

For a long time, Morgan simply sat and stared at it, trying to absorb what it meant. For the woman he was looking at was a complete stranger. Slowly, he let the paper fall to the desk, his mind whirling. Then he reread Farley's report.

It was clear that this woman, the real Isadora Van Harte, had indeed left for Bermuda on that fateful flight. 'And that's when the switch must have been made,' he murmured to himself. 'It had to be.'

Quickly he cast his mind back. Elizabeth had been informed about the crash and the survival of her niece by a high-ranking police official that she knew socially. He'd also called Morgan and told him, and Morgan had gone at once to Hartelands to pick her up and take her to the hospital.

The question was, how had *whoever she was* been misidentified? She'd been unconscious at the time – that he knew.

The bracelet. Of course, he remembered now. The coastguards who'd found her had mentioned it to a doctor who'd checked the passenger manifesto, and unsurprisingly had found only one woman called Isadora. But how had she come to be wearing Isadora's bracelet in the first place? Had she stolen it? And why, when she'd woken up in the hospital with everyone calling her by another woman's name, hadn't she told them the truth?

Morgan shook his head. He was being a fool. There could only be one explanation – she knew that Isadora's aunt was rich, and she was hoping to cash in.

Morgan got to his feet and began to pace. He didn't even know her name. He was in love with a woman, a thief, a liar, and who knew what the hell else, and he didn't even know her name! Rage, pain and a nameless fear began to boil deep inside him.

* * *

'I'm just off then, poppet,' Elizabeth called through to the garden, and Imogen, lazing beneath the trees in a hammock, looked up and waved.

'All right. Have a good time!'

'I will. We always enjoy playing at Talulah's. Her cook makes the most divine Martinis,' Elizabeth called back, her eyes twinkling. 'Chance, is the car ready?'

They'd just turned the corner at the bottom of the road when Morgan pulled up outside the bungalow and slammed the door shut. He stalked into the foyer, then through the main lounge, spotting the white hammock gently swinging under the trees through the French windows. With long, rapid strides he crossed the lawn, Imogen sensing rather than seeing him approach. She let her book, *Under Milk Wood* by Dylan Thomas, fall from her fingers as she met his eyes.

The look on his face was . . .

She yelped as, without breaking his stride, he reached down and literally yanked her from the hammock. She was wearing a yellow and black sarong-type skirt and a matching yellow blouse, tied in a knot at the midriff. Her long black hair was loose and cascaded around her as she was jerked into the air.

'Morgan!' she cried, feeling his fingers bite into her rib-cage as he swung her up and around, landing her hard on her feet in front of him.

'Who the hell are you, lady?' he snarled.

Imogen froze, her eyes growing enormous. 'Wh-wh-what do you mean?' she stammered.

Ruthlessly he shook her, making her dark tresses fly and then settle, clinging to her cheeks and neck and arms. 'Don't lie to me. You're no more Isadora Van Harte than I am!' He watched her face drain of all colour, and knew he should be feeling triumphant, but instead felt only sick at heart. 'Yes, I thought that would take the wind out of your sails.'

Imogen could only continue to stare at him mutely. She'd grown so used to her other identity now that she'd forgotten how tenuous it was. 'H-how did you find out?' she managed.

Morgan's eyes narrowed impatiently. 'Does it matter? I had a private investigator check out the real Isadora Van Harte. She died in the plane crash, didn't she?'

Imogen felt her throat clench with tears. Isadora, laughing and ordering another drink. Isadora, so afraid of flying. She felt herself being shaken again. 'Stop it!' she yelled, beginning to feel angry. 'Yes, she died in the plane crash. They all died, damn you!'

Morgan's fingers tightened, then relaxed. Whatever else she was, whatever else she'd done, or planned to do, the nightmare of that plane crash would haunt her for the rest of her life. He knew that. 'How come you were wearing her bracelet?' he asked, more gently now.

Imogen sighed. 'It fell off on the way over. The turbulence, I suppose. And she kept fiddling with it. She was scared of flying. By then, we were all a little nervous. The lightning—'

'So it fell off,' he kept her ruthlessly to the point. 'Did you take the opportunity to palm it then?'

Imogen blinked. 'What?' she asked numbly.

Oh so innocent, he thought. And he wanted to believe her. Even now. She looked so lovely, flushed with the sun, wide-eyed, her hair clinging to her. 'The bracelet,' he snarled. 'How did it get onto your wrist?'

'We tried to get it back on Isadora's wrist, but it had a complicated clasp. I couldn't do it up. So she put it on mine and showed me how to do it, and then the plane went down and oh, *what does a stupid bracelet matter now*!' she yelled. 'Isadora's dead. I only knew her for a short time, but I liked her. We talked. She told me about her aunt, and how she'd lost her mother just like I—'

'Oh yes, her aunt,' Morgan was so overwhelmed with his conflicting emotions that he was in no mood to listen to reason. 'That was very convenient, wasn't it?' he asked. And as she continued to stare at him with those innocent, puzzled blue eyes he shook her again. 'Wasn't it!'

Imogen had had enough. She kicked out, connecting with his shin. Morgan yelped and instinctively let go of her.

She turned to flee, but he was far too quick. With a forward hop, his leg still stinging, he grabbed her and they fell onto the cool green grass. Imogen struggled wildly, but it was hopeless. Soon she was flat on her back and he was lying atop her, her hands pinioned to the grass either side of her head, his fingers curled hard around her wrists.

Even as she struggled, her body was aware of his closeness. The scent of the shampoo in his hair. The touch of their bare skin where his legs lay over hers. Her heart began to beat fast, and for a totally different reason than fear. She went limp with despair.

Even when he was attacking her, accusing her, she couldn't help but want him. What was wrong with her?

'That's better,' he rasped as she went still beneath him. 'Now, tell me. When did you hatch your plan? Was it in the hospital, when you realised that everyone thought you were Isadora?'

Imogen blinked, trying to sort out the whole mess. 'Plan?' she echoed. Had he found out who she really was? Did he know about her plans to find Robbie's killer?

'Come on!' he snarled, his face so close to hers she could feel his breath on her cheek. 'The plan to fleece Elizabeth.'

Imogen's thoughts ground to a halt. 'Elizabeth?' And then she understood.

Morgan laughed harshly. 'My word, you're good. To look at you, anyone would think I'd just dealt you a mortal blow.'

Imogen closed her eyes, unable to bear the look on his face. To love someone who didn't love you back was painful enough, but to love someone who actively loathed you! She didn't know it, but two huge, heart-broken tears squeezed out of her eyes and trickled down the sides of her face, falling into her hair. Morgan, watching them, felt something hard and brutal grasp his own heart and give it a wrench. Just in case he should forget that he loved her. And that he couldn't hurt her without hurting himself.

He dragged in a shaken breath. 'Look at me,' he said, a touch of defeat already sounding in his voice.

Miserably, Imogen did so, her blue eyes awash. 'I love Elizabeth,' she said simply. 'I wouldn't do anything to hurt her.'

Morgan laughed. She sounded so sincere! 'Oh no? You think pretending to be her only relative, her long-lost niece, doesn't qualify as hurting her?'

'It was partly because of her that I didn't speak out at once!' Imogen cried. 'I heard the nurses talking about her heart condition. They said it might have killed her if her niece hadn't survived.'

Morgan shook his head, admiring her gall even as he hated her for it. 'Oh, I see,' he said sarcastically. 'So you took on Isadora's persona to save Elizabeth the pain! Do you expect me to believe that?' he gritted. 'Well, do you?' he all but shouted.

Imogen flinched. 'No. I meant to tell the doctor when we were alone so that he could break it to her gently. But then . . .'

Then Tony Jackson's two goons had showed up, looking for her. And she knew she was in danger. And she'd been scared.

But she couldn't tell Morgan any of that, she realised. She and Ellis had agreed that it would be best to continue their subterfuge until they'd managed to get enough evidence on Tony Jackson to convict him. By telling Morgan about it she would be dumping Ellis in it. He'd confessed to her that he hadn't told Averil anything, and Morgan would feel honour-bound to tell his sister all that he knew.

Besides, if she told Morgan, she knew he'd also feel honour-bound to take on Tony Jackson himself. She understood him well enough by now to know that. And she just couldn't pit him against Tony Jackson. From what Ellis had told her, Jackson was dangerous. A murderously dangerous sewer rat. And the thought of him killing Morgan . . .

'But then?' he prompted, having watched the expressions cross her face with fascination. 'Come on, what's going on in that treacherous little mind of yours now?'

Imogen swallowed hard. 'Nothing,' she said weakly. 'I can't tell you.'

Morgan's grip on her wrists tightened warningly. 'You will tell me,' he gritted. 'You'll tell me everything. Or else.'

Imogen took a ragged breath. She was tired of all this bullying. His body seemed to be pressing her into the earth, and she could feel her loins melting. Her breasts hardening. How long before he noticed what he was doing to her? And the humiliation then . . . She wouldn't be able to stand it. If he looked down on her with contempt now, what would he think of her when he realised how easily he could have her?

'Or else what, Morgan?' she tried to put as much bite and sneering challenge into her voice as she could possibly muster. 'You'll tell Elizabeth?' She laughed bitterly. 'But you can't can you? You know as well as I do if you tell her now you'll bring on an attack. You'll kill her,' she said flatly.

Morgan paled. 'You cold, heartless little—'

Don't say it! her mind wailed. *Please, don't say it.* Imogen began to struggle again. 'Let me up, damn you.' She strained against him but it was futile. She slumped back, defeated.

Morgan was thinking furiously. She was right, of course. He couldn't tell Elizabeth anything. Not yet, anyway. But that didn't mean she'd won. Hell no.

'What's your name?' he asked suddenly, taking them both by surprise.

Imogen stared mutely up at him. Once she'd longed to hear him speak her name out loud, but now, she knew, it could never be. Not until she and Ellis had Jackson behind bars.

'Just call me Isadora,' she said tiredly. But it was the worst thing she could have said.

Morgan's self-control snapped. 'I'll be damned if I will,' he snarled. And his head swooped.

The instant their lips touched, both of them were lost. Imogen felt the force and pressure of his punishing kiss push her lips open, and at the same time other floodgates burst. She felt molten-hot heat flood her from the inside out. His hands moved from her wrists and down her body, his fingers encountering the sensitive skin on her waist. He reached up, cupping her breasts through the thin blouse, his thumbs finding her erect nipples and rubbing over them, making them ache painfully.

Imogen moaned beneath his lips.

Her hands, free now, reached up to run along his broad shoulders, and down, over his back, her fingers reaching out either side of his spine. Morgan's lips slewed from her face and down the side of her neck, along the cords of her taut throat to the valley between her breasts. His mouth pressed against each of them in turn, sucking her nipples through the thinness of her blouse, making her arch her back instinctively. Her hands moved across his taut buttocks, gripping convulsively. Morgan cried out hoarsely. He was so hard now, he felt as if he would explode.

'Morgan, oh, Morgan,' she moaned, and he went to cry out her own name . . . and froze.

Because he didn't know what it was.

She felt him tense, sensed his sudden withdrawal, both in mind and body, and released a brief, hard, sharp cry of bitter regret. Her eyes shot open and saw the shuttered, dangerous look which crossed his face and shut her out, as securely as an iron door.

Breathing heavily, he got first to his knees and then to his feet, and for a long moment stood towering over her, looking down at her. Her lips were sore from the fierceness of his kiss. Her body was trembling. He wanted her so much he thought he could die of it.

'Be careful, *Isadora*,' he gritted. 'From now on, be very, very careful.'

And he turned and left her.

Imogen watched him go, her body still on fire but her mind in despair. 'Oh, Morgan,' she said softly, fresh tears spilling from her eyes. 'Oh, Morgan, I love you.'

But she was careful to only whisper it, so that he couldn't hear her.

THIRTEEN

Averil heard the dim shout, 'Ahoy there, landlubber!' and raised a hand to shield her eyes. She'd just left a meeting of the BHDC (Bermudan Holidays for Disabled Children), of which she was chairman and founder. She'd set it up several years ago in order to enable disabled children from poor backgrounds throughout the world to come to Bermuda for a holiday. Since she'd never had any real desire to become a business tycoon like her brother, or just laze her days away doing nothing specific, like a lot of her friends, she'd long since decided to work more or less full time for charities.

She lobbied her brother and Elizabeth constantly and mercilessly, but neither seemed to mind. Now, still thinking how best to persuade the Romanian authorities to let several children come to Bermuda next year, she was sitting outside at one of the harbour-front cafés when she heard herself being hailed.

She walked a little way down the paved road, towards the vast flotilla of private boats, and squinted into the sun. Instantly she recognised the sails of the *Sea Siren*, Tony Jackson's impressive yacht. It was Tony himself, standing on the deck, who'd called her. 'We're just out for a sail to Grassy Bay,' he called. 'Fancy coming along?'

Averil smiled. 'We're still speaking then?' she asked, somewhat wryly. Tony had been avoiding her ever since she'd told him it was over between them, but if he'd got over the sulks, she could see no good reason to decline his gracious offer. After all, it was a lovely day.

'Of course we are, *cara mia*,' Tony spread his hands elegantly. 'I've got iced champagne and fresh strawberries.'

'Well, that does it then,' she called back, laughing.

Tony spoke rapidly to one of his crew, and a few minutes later a small powerboat edged her way. Averil got in, and when they arrived back she reached out to take Tony's hand as he helped her climb up the ladder and aboard the yacht itself. He was dressed only in shorts and canvas shoes.

'Tony, it's nice to see you again,' she said, smiling at him with genuine warmth. She hated to quarrel with anyone – even someone as thick-skinned as she suspected Tony was.

For his part, Tony watched her closely, and nodded to himself at her spontaneous greeting. He was right to suspect that she knew nothing about this diamond affair – which meant she was still salvageable.

'I'll tell the captain to get underway then,' he said.

'How is Olaf?' she asked dryly, remembering the dour Scandinavian captain from previous jaunts.

Tony grinned. 'You know, I swear he secretly resents it whenever I ask him to take me out.'

Averil laughed, but as soon as Tony returned, the motor began to churn. 'Just to get us out of the harbour,' Tony explained, looking up at the sails. 'There's enough wind to get us to Grassy Bay. I much prefer wind power to diesel, don't you?'

Averil nodded and leaned against the rail with a small sigh. She couldn't help but wish it was Ellis by her side, and was determined to be extra nice to Tony because of it.

As they pulled out of the harbour, leaving Albury's Point Ferry Terminal slowly behind, she looked across at Tony speculatively. She'd have to introduce him to Ellis, of course. They probably wouldn't like each other, but still, you had to be civilised about things like this. And Bermuda was such a small island. Although, she suddenly thought, she might not be staying here much longer. Ellis, as he'd made clear, had a life in Amsterdam. And she couldn't imagine him leaving the islands without her.

She supposed she'd miss all this. As the crew began to silently and competently set about the sails, the wind flapping the canvas, she felt the sleek boat begin to surge through the water and felt just a twinge of sadness. As they sailed through Two Rock Passage, with the islands of Hawkins, Long, Ports and Nelly off to the west, she knew she was going to miss this island paradise of hers.

But Europe beckoned. And with Ellis by her side, who knew what adventures lay ahead? Rome in summer, Paris in spring. And diamonds to learn about. How could she regret such a fascinating future?

'Penny for your thoughts, *cara*,' Tony interrupted, looking at her curiously.

Averil glanced at him and shrugged. 'Oh, nothing special,' she lied. Just then a steward approached.

'There is a radio message for you, Mr Jackson, sir,' he said quietly.

Tony, who'd been slowly sidling up the rail closer and closer to Averil, looked at him impatiently. 'Not now, Marco. Take a message.'

The steward, a young dark-haired boy, glanced at Averil then apologetically back to his employer. 'It is your friend from Naples, sir. He said he wanted just a quick word.'

Averil glanced casually across the Great Sound towards the furthermost north point of Great Bermuda itself.

'Very well. I won't be long, *cara*. Help yourself to champagne,' he added, taking the opportunity to lift one of her hands to his mouth and kiss the knuckles. Averil smiled. Trust Tony! He always had to be the suave one.

Tony went forward to the small radio room, and she, as suggested, went below to the galley for the champagne. She found it in the fridge, and popped the cork carefully, holding it over the sink in case of spillages. She looked up as, through the open porthole, she heard Tony's voice. The *Sea Siren* was not a huge boat, but had always seemed big enough to her. Now she realised how very compact it was, as Tony's voice, even from the radio room, carried to her.

'No, I told your associate at the time. The package on the plane I wanted picked up never arrived.'

Averil shrugged, and reached up to the cupboard above her, looking for champagne flutes. She had never been much of an entrepreneur's daughter, and didn't take much notice even of Morgan when he talked business. She found two glasses and stood them on the pretty blue-marbled worktop.

'But I *did* pay you. Yes, yes, the going rate for specialised work. If that thieving little guttersnipe you use told you differently then you'd better have another word with him.'

Averil poured the frothing liquid, patiently waiting for the foaming white head to subside.

'No, that was something else entirely. I no longer need transportation for the ice.'

Averil filled the glasses to the top and carefully scooped them up. She walked back to the open deck, the wind and sails, the crying seagulls and the deep-blue ocean and vast sky. She didn't think much about Tony's somewhat mysterious conversation then. But later she would.

When it was far too late.

* * *

Feeling restless and on edge, Imogen walked through the cool marble foyer of Elizabeth's house and hoped she was having a good nap. She'd finally persuaded her to get into the habit of taking a siesta after lunch, a fact that both Grace and Elizabeth's doctor thanked her for profusely.

Now, though, she felt strangely lonely without Elizabeth to talk to. Over the weeks, she'd come to think of her as a real aunt. They could and did talk about anything and everything – from literature (Elizabeth arguing the cause of the American writers, Imogen defending the British) to politics, garden design and even the Bermuda Triangle! Now she approached the library with a vague desire to take her mind off things with a good book.

She knew it wouldn't work, of course. Every time her mind found an idle moment, images of Morgan filled it. She'd tried dislodging him by discreetly pumping Robbie's friends (mostly women), but so far, nobody had been able to give her a hint as to how Robbie had fallen foul of Tony Jackson.

Restlessly, she searched the bookshelves, trying to forget the look of contempt in Morgan's eyes as he'd looked down at her. Dammit, she must stop thinking about that!

Her fingers roved along the colourful book spines and suddenly stopped as a title caught her eye. *The Legend of Zorro.* One of Robbie's all-time favourites as a boy.

Instantly she could remember one summer holiday in Devon, long ago. They'd been with . . . yes, their father, one of the few times she'd ever stayed with him for any length of time. He'd rented a holiday cottage near a farm for two weeks.

She had warm memories of feeding an old donkey a carrot, and watching, wide-eyed, as a calf had been born. Robbie had thought it really gross, with all the blood and stuff. But she'd been fascinated. And then days by the river, with Robbie wielding a sword and making the ragged 'Z' mark in the dusty ground. Imogen, perforce, had had to be the baddie, the awful Don . . . what was it Robbie had called her? Don Blackheart. Or some such name. And at night, when they were supposed to be asleep, he'd sneak into her room with a torch and read her the latest chapter.

Now Imogen pulled the book from the ledge, and saw with a smile of delight that even the cover was the same as she remembered from that long-ago time. Obviously a first edition. She smiled down at the masked man on the front, with his black and scarlet cape and glittering sword.

Oh, Robbie! She walked with it to her bedroom and sat on the bed, staring down at the cover. Quickly she opened it and began to read. And as she did so, she felt something monumental shift in the back of her mind. Like a vast, important boulder being rolled away from a cave that would tell her something hugely important.

And then she could hear Robbie's voice – not the voice of the man he'd become, but the child he'd been. High, and excited. 'Sis, sis, listen. I've just thought up this amazing code.'

'It isn't Morse, is it?' her own childish voice answered, all those years ago. 'You know I can't remember Morse.'

'No, twit head,' Robbie had responded, with his usual careless insult. 'It's much better than Morse. Look, this is how it goes. You choose a book, right. Like *Zorro.* And you read it until you find a word that you want. Then you see what the word after it is in the book. Then you write that word down – instead of the one you really want. See? So to somebody who doesn't know what book you started out with it's just a load of old gobbledygook. But when you look them up in *Zorro*, and see what the word next to it is – abracadabra, you've got a message you can understand. Look, I'll show you what I mean.'

Imogen jumped as she heard a thump, and realised she'd dropped the book. She stared down at it blankly for several moments, then quickly jumped up and ran to her wardrobe. Extracting her brother's last letter to her, she hurried with it to the table and spread it out, grabbing a pen and notebook. Then she went back to fetch the *Zorro* book.

Her heart thundering, and feeling slightly sick with excitement, she opened the first page, and then looked at her brother's letter. The first word which was written in darker ink was 'forget'.

Feverishly, she began to read the first page of the *Zorro* book. Nowhere did she see the word 'forget' so she hastily turned the page. And instantly saw it. The word before it was 'I'.

She wrote it down on the pad and checked her brother's letter again. The next word written in darker ink was 'shade'.

It was on page five of the *Zorro* book that she found it. The word before that was 'hidden'. She wrote that down.

For the next hour and a half she worked steadily between the two documents, until, at the end, she finally had Robbie's hidden message to her. Obviously he'd suspected Tony Jackson was having his mail intercepted, which was why he'd written it in code. Had he suspected, even then, that something awful might happen to him? She felt tears threaten her and hastily pushed them aside, concentrating instead on the all-important message. Of course it was in very bad English, but perfectly understandable. And totally amazing.

For, unless she had gone totally crazy, it told her that Robbie had hidden treasure in a cave near Five Star Island.

Quickly, feeling almost light-headed with excitement and shock, she hunted out one of Elizabeth's books on the island, and from a map saw that Five Star Island, far from being remote or secret, lay only a little way off the main coastline of south Bermuda itself, just off the parish called Southampton. From the map, there were two shipwrecks near there, the *Emma Davis* and the *Norkoplin*.

But surely, Imogen thought, he wouldn't have hidden the treasure (which she now knew was Ellis's stolen diamonds) so close to shore. And at a regular and well-known diving spot, too.

Or had he been doubly clever, reasoning that no one would expect him to do just that? Namely, Tony Jackson.

Quickly she ran to her telephone extension and picked it up, dialling Ellis's phone number. After three rings it was picked up, and she was just about to launch into an excited voice when she heard the recorded message on his voicemail. By the time she'd listened to him remind her to leave her name and number she'd had a chance to at least gather her thoughts. She could hardly blurt out what she knew over the phone. Not with Tony Jackson around. Ellis had warned her that he had spies and connections everywhere on the island.

When the tone bleeped in her ear, all she said was, in a tight, strained voice, 'Ellis, it's me. Im—Isadora. I need to see you right away. It's urgent. Very urgent. I'm at home.' And she hung up. Nothing in that, surely, to give much of the game away if anyone who happened to have big ears had overheard it.

But oh how she wished Ellis had been in!

Restlessly, she began to pace. Reread, yet again, the deciphered message. It said that where the diamonds were hidden you had to go through a tunnel beneath the rocks to find them, but that there was a cave which opened out after only a few feet.

It sounded daunting. Robbie, as a skilled and experienced diver, wouldn't have thought anything of exploring underwater caves. She could just imagine him finding it. Perhaps, if it was big enough, even hauling himself out of the water and exploring it with a big flashlight.

Restlessly, she tried Ellis's number again. There was still no answer. She paced some more. Heard Elizabeth beginning to stir. Checked her watch. Imagined her brother's excited face as he swam out to his cave to hide his stash of gems. Could even imagine him laughing and planning how to spend it – on wine, women and song, no doubt.

And then dying because of it. Someone had either tampered with his equipment, bleeding his tanks dangerously low on air, or Tony Jackson's hitmen had followed him down and simply held him under until he . . .

Abruptly, she stopped her thoughts right there. Phoned Ellis again. Could have cried when she got only his voicemail. 'Dammit, Ellis, where are you?' she muttered.

She heard Elizabeth leave her bedroom and head for the kitchen. Ominously, her head began to ache. And she knew she just couldn't wait any longer. Ellis or no Ellis, she simply had to see for herself.

* * *

Getting off the bus near Dax Diving, Imogen cursed her lack of contacts. She'd rather have gone to any place but this, but Dax's was the only place she knew. But she was in luck. As she approached it she could see that a big launch was docked with a large crowd of people milling around, suiting up.

'Something good happening?' she asked, as she oh so casually approached them and turned to the first woman she met.

'I'll say. We're going to watch some shark-feeding off East Whale Bay. It's not dangerous though,' she quickly added, more to convince herself, Imogen was sure, than anyone else. 'Are you coming with us?'

She was about to say no when she suddenly realised what a heaven-sent opportunity this was. There were only two Dax employees that she could see, both of them toiling hard to hand out the equipment from a big storage locker, and obviously not counting the numbers as they did so. No doubt they did that later, right before they dived. 'I sure am,' she said at once, and stood in line.

She didn't really expect to get away with it, and, on a smaller expedition, she was sure she wouldn't have, but when it was her turn she was given all the equipment she needed – except a torch. It was fair enough, she supposed. You didn't need a torch out in the open sea to watch sharks!

Looking around her, feeling like a thief, she surreptitiously stashed her ill-gotten gains behind a big rubbish bin and made her way back into town. She had little difficulty buying a powerful underwater torch, but even as she made her way back to the diving school she wondered what her next move could be.

As she'd expected, the dock was now deserted, the shark-seekers having long gone. She had all the equipment she needed, but no boat. And before a Dax diver would take her out, he'd ask for proof of her competence.

She walked back to the diving school, on the verge of tearing her hair out in sheer frustration. She watched restlessly as a small launch came in, watching the man at the tiller steer it and then cut the simple engine. He tied it off.

She walked slowly towards him, nodding absently as he passed her on the way to the office. She tried her best to look the humble, disinterested sightseer. Then walked rapidly to the edge of the dock and stood looking down into the boat. It had one of those motors which you started by pulling on the handle. You steered it, she'd noticed, by simply pointing the boat in the direction you wanted to go. Surely anybody could do that?

She walked back past the big storage locker to the bins and picked up her gear. It was while she was out of sight behind the locker that she heard a car pull in and froze. But after the sound of the door slamming there was a reassuring silence, and she nervously glanced around.

The Jaguar! Instantly, she recognised it. Damn! Just her rotten luck. Or was it? He was obviously inside the office. If she stole the boat – no, *borrowed* the boat – it wouldn't really matter, would it? Not to someone like him. His company had so many boats. Besides, she'd bring it back. Time then to face the music.

She was being reckless and stupid and she knew it, but she also found herself beyond caring. She'd had the foresight to buy a big map of the islands along with the torch and the navigation looked simple enough. Due south-east from the harbour, detour north of Hinson's Island, and then past Darrell's and Burt Island and south to the long flat stretch that made up south Bermuda. There would be buoys and markers, she was sure. It couldn't be *that* difficult – not when you could actually see with the naked eye where you needed to go! And it was not as if she was going out into open ocean. If she got into trouble, there would be many eyes about to notice her distress.

With a grim feeling of fatalism, which was oddly comforting, she tossed her gear into the boat. As she did so, Morgan, who'd just accepted a beer from the boat's pilot, walked to the window of the office and stood poised, the beer bottle halfway angled to his lips. He recognised her at once, of course; the long black braid of hair snaking down her back was unmistakable. What took him a little longer to register was the gear she was flinging into the boat. But then he realised: air tanks. He swore.

'Phil, is the speedboat in dock?' he snapped quickly.

'Sure. It's not due out for another hour. Hey, where are you going, boss?' But Morgan was already gone, sprinting down the quay, where a sleek turquoise and white boat was tied up, bobbing on the gentle waves. As he reached for the mooring rope, he heard the engine of the other boat start up.

He only hoped she knew what she was doing.

He leapt down into his own boat and started the engine. At least it was a very calm day, with no bad weather forecast. That was something. And he'd be right on her tail, all the way. Wherever she was going. But when he caught up with her he was going to make her wish she'd never been born. Of all the crazy, stupid things to do . . .

He found himself admiring her courage and spirit, even as his heart beat sickeningly with fear for her. 'Damn you, Isadora, or whatever the hell your name is,' he shouted, but by now there was no one to hear him but the seagulls.

FOURTEEN

Her heart in her mouth, Imogen set off across Hamilton Harbour. Checking the map, she could only hope that the first big island she was approaching was in fact Hinson's Island, and not one of the others. Deep in her heart she knew what she was doing was almost criminally stupid, but she was reassured by the constant presence of other boats. The ferries, the pleasure craft, the parasailers and jet-skiers. The day remained mercifully calm, with barely a chop on the protected waters of Great Sound and Little Sound, both being nearly encircled by the main island of Bermuda itself.

With the passage between Hinson's Island and two others finally behind her, she began to relax a little now that she was heading back towards the southern stretch of the mainland. She didn't notice, amid all the other sea traffic, the turquoise and white boat keeping right off her stern and in visual contact.

She almost began to relax and enjoy herself. She'd hardly have been human if she hadn't found it at least a little exhilarating. She was, after all, merely a humble secretary from Oxfordshire, and yet now she was piloting her own purloined boat towards Little Sound off Bermuda, in order to recover stolen diamonds. It was hardly something that happened to a girl every day! Only a nagging doubt about her ability to complete the dive, and the very real dangers it presented, kept her from laughing out loud in sheer delight.

A water-skier shot past off her port bow and waved at her cheerfully. Nervously taking her hand off the unfamiliar tiller, she waved back. Her throat was dry, her heart beating just a little too fast for comfort. Let's face it, she thought wryly, she was hardly a daredevil!

Behind her, Morgan tried to figure out where she was heading, and why it was so damned important that she had to steal one of his boats and some of his diving gear. The thought of calling in the cops and letting her be arrested was so sweet he could almost taste it. But the thought of visiting her behind bars tightened his body into an almost unbearable ache.

He carefully slowed the speedboat down as Imogen's boat also slowed. Imogen had, in fact, only done this in order to get her bearings. The vast acreage of greenery now lying off to her left had to be . . . She checked the map again. Yes, Riddell's Bay Golf Course. She powered up again, getting used to handling the boat now and gaining in confidence.

She carefully followed the coastline of Warwick Parish, past three small islands she didn't know the names of, and then suddenly, she was there. The small island coming up simply *had* to be Five Star Island. Somewhat to her relief, there was already a big boat near her, and as she got closer, she could see that it was one of those big, glass-bottomed boats which allowed tourists to look down into the mysteries and beauties of the sea without actually getting wet.

As she drew closer, she almost laughed out loud. It was a Dax Leisure boat.

Morgan, too, recognised one of his own craft, but it only puzzled him all the more. Had she stolen a boat merely to take a joyride from one side of the island to the other? He powered down, and, when he was sure she had stopped, took the opportunity to put the big flat-bottomed boat between them.

Still utterly puzzled, he began to get into the diving gear stashed in the boat's locker. Because he was more experienced, Morgan was already in position as Imogen rolled backwards into the water.

All the time she'd been suiting up she'd been berating herself. Here there was no Morgan to tie a rope to her and be there if she got into trouble. No Skinny waiting in the boat to raise the alarm if something should go wrong. But she'd gone on putting on the wetsuit and checking her equipment, and now, with a cooling rush, she was in the waters of Little Sound. For a moment she simply let herself get used to it all over again. Breathed, and let herself trust her gear. And then, with a remembered thrust of her flippers, she set off.

She found the first shipwreck easily. There was even a pair of divers already exploring it. She knew if they spotted her they'd be worried because she had no 'buddy', and so gave it a wide berth.

Her brother's instructions were, of course, burned into her memory. And now that she was here, actively searching for the gems which had got him killed, she began to feel as if a great pressure was being lifted off her. At that moment, nothing would have persuaded her she was doing wrong. It was almost as if she could feel Robbie beginning to rest in peace at last.

She checked her depth gauge, and was relieved to see how little she had had to come down. It really was shallow here.

She came upon the first coral reef and wall of rock almost before she knew it. She stopped, once more awed by the darting fish, the colourful shrimps, the nervous crabs. But she had to go past the first reef, she remembered.

Behind her, careful to keep her in view at all times, Morgan followed.

Don't get too excited, Imogen reminded herself. You breathe too much air that way. Like an evil little genie perched on her shoulder, she suddenly remembered Morgan telling her about all the hazards of diving. Exhaustion, burst lung, air embolisms, spontaneous pneumothorax, subcutaneous emphysema, the niggles and skin bends. Even decompression sickness. None of which, she firmly reminded herself, affected shallow-water divers. But it was one thing to know that and another not to worry about them!

No, the nasty little genie said. Better to worry about the things which really *could* happen to you. Seasickness, for example – something which sounded so silly, and yet could kill you if you began to choke on your own vomit.

Imogen shook her head, angry at herself. Behind her, Morgan wondered what the hell she was doing. Where was she going? There was nothing here to be seen. She'd headed away from the shipwrecks, and this reef was nothing special. And yet he was sure she wouldn't be doing this out of sheer craziness. She was up to something, and he wanted to know what it was.

Meanwhile, Imogen's little genie began to chant gleefully once more. Hypothermia, ear squeeze, sinus squeeze, mask squeeze. She fought the desire to touch her mask. It was fine. The seal was fine. Just take slow, deep breaths, she told herself. You can't panic now, for pity's sake. Not now!

And then she saw it.

Her brother's directions had been conveyed in totally clear, if rather idiosyncratic English. There, right in front of her, was the big 'pregnant' rock. And it did indeed look like a woman's bulging stomach. Underneath it, the decoded message said, was the entrance to the cave. No wonder very few people knew about it. How many divers would bother to go to the sea bottom just at this point? All the interesting stuff, the coral and the fish, was above her.

Slowly, she remembered how to let herself sink. As she went down, she checked her depth gauge nervously, mightily relieved to see that she still wasn't at any great depth, but her breathing rate soared nonetheless. And, right on cue, her little companion began to come up with all the breathing hazards Morgan had told her about. Oxygen poisoning, nitrogen narcosis, hypoxia and anoxia. It was a testimony to her total determination that Imogen thrust them all away.

OK, so she was no action woman. But she was coping all right. And then she saw the narrow black entrance, the absence of daylight, and wondered. For what felt like a long while, she simply lay there, lightly resting on the sea floor and looking in. Then, numbly, she felt her hand move, and watched it unhook the big underwater flashlight from her belt. She switched it on, and a beam of bright light shone through the tunnel. It was short, Robbie had said. Only a few feet.

She could do that. Of course she could. Just go.

Behind her, keeping the bulging rock between them so that he was looking down on just her ankles and flippers, Morgan began to worry. She was so still. Had something gone wrong? Was she in trouble?

A sudden, ugly thought shot through him. Had she come out here to commit suicide? He had no idea what kind of trouble she might be in. What she was mixed up with. He began to push away from the rock, wanting only to go to her, to make her safe, to promise her anything, and then the flippers disappeared. For a second he jerked comically in the water, then he dived, just in time to see her flashlight bouncing off the walls of the tunnel.

He hadn't known it was there. For all the years he'd been diving in these waters, he had never heard anybody mention it. He shook his head, then felt a huge wave of anger crash over him. What the hell did she, an absolute beginner, think she was doing cave diving for pity's sake? Didn't she have any idea how disorientating it could be? Or how claustrophobic? Or even, if the system of caves and tunnels was complex, how easy it was to get lost? He remembered once diving through some caves with an expert guide; how they'd come across the remains of a sea turtle lying on the bottom. Even that ocean-wise animal had got lost and, being an air-breather, had finally drowned.

Without hesitation, or a torch of his own, he went in after her.

Ahead, unaware of her faithful tracker, Imogen tried not to think about where she was. Surrounded by rock. Totally submerged in water. In a strange place, reliant on a torch and air tanks for her very life.

It was just as well that, as soon as she'd turned a bend, she could see the dim glow of some ambient light. Robbie's cave must have a crack in it somewhere which went all the way to the top and let in daylight. She could almost have wept with relief as she swam quickly towards it, trying not to think of the return journey through that spooky, tomb-like tunnel.

She surfaced a few minutes later and found herself in a large, domed cave. There were no fantastic stalagmites or stalactites. No gently sloping shore. Not even much dancing, sea-reflected light, but enough to enable her to see and clamber out clumsily onto a large, flat section of rock. She took off her mask and gulped 'normal' air gratefully.

She was shaking. Until then, she hadn't realised the toll she was taking on her body's nervous system. Her knees felt like rubber. But she was here!

She stood up, easing off her tanks and carefully placing them where they couldn't fall back into the sea, very mindful that they were – literally – her lifeline.

According to Robbie's letter, the stones were hidden under a 'mound of weeds'. She clambered upwards, the movement covering the sound of Morgan surfacing just behind and below her.

Morgan watched her, narrow-eyed in the dim light, as she clambered up the rocks. With ease, he pulled himself up after her, the strength of his upper body allowing him to do so with far more dignity than Imogen. He too stashed his tanks, checking that both of them had more than enough air to get back out again. Then, he followed, carefully checking every toe hold before he did so.

How had she known this place was here? Had she been to the islands before?

Imogen found the pile of dried and browning seaweed by default – she stepped on it. By now she was on a flat, high stretch of rock, and she knelt down with ease, her heart sounding like a drum in her head as she pushed the seaweed apart and delved in.

Instantly, her hands felt something hard and yet yielding, and a moment later she withdrew a small drawstring bag of what seemed like suede. It was wrapped in a polythene bag. For a long moment, she simply stared down at it, then unwrapped the plastic bag.

She felt cold now. As cold as the stones which she knew it contained. She reached for her torch, and, awkwardly positioning it under her arm, angled it down onto her hand. Loosening the drawstring she tipped out a little river of sparkling light onto her hand.

Diamonds. Sparkling, glittering diamonds.

'What the hell?'

The voice made her scream. She turned, dropping the white, shining stones onto the ground around her, where they rolled along the hard dark rock like pulsating, living things.

Imogen shone the light on Morgan's face with utter disbelief. 'Morgan,' she breathed. 'Morgan?' For a moment she wondered if she was simply seeing things. As if her imagination and need had conjured him up out of thin air.

'This is what it's all about?' Morgan asked, looking down at the nearly full bag in her hand and then at the scattered stones around her. Those that caught the beam of the torch's light glittered like animal eyes in the darkness of a jungle night. Suddenly he was reminded of the Beatles song 'Lucy in the Sky with Diamonds'.

She looked so breathtakingly lovely.

'What are you doing here?' she asked, dumbfounded.

'I followed you,' he said simply, reaching down and picking up the nearest stone to him. 'It is a diamond, I take it?' he asked, almost conversationally. After the events of the last hour or so, he felt as if nothing could surprise him.

'Yes,' Imogen said, struggling to get her mind around all of this. 'You saw me take the boat?'

'And the gear. I was on your tail from the time you left the harbour. I must admit, I never knew this place existed. But you've obviously been here before.'

Mutely, Imogen shook her head. Morgan. Here. Right in front of her. The rubber wetsuit moulding his chest and thighs. She wanted . . . She swayed, and gently let herself sink to the rocky floor. 'I've done it,' she said at last, slowly and in wonder. 'Robbie, I've done it.'

'You sure have,' Morgan said dryly, looking down at her clenched hand. 'They're stolen, of course.'

'What?' Imogen said vaguely, then followed his gaze down to the suede bag in her hand. 'Oh, yes,' she admitted.

So she was a thief. He'd always known it must be something like that. And a jewel thief no less. How glamorous! He supposed he should feel something. Disgust. Disappointment. Something. But he felt none of those things. 'How did you do it?' he asked instead.

Imogen looked up at him. Her braid had come loose, and her hair clung to her damp cheeks. In the torchlight, her face was a vision of ghostly planes and angles. 'Do what?'

'Steal them.'

Imogen shook her head. 'I didn't. They belong to Ellis,' she said simply. 'I'm going to give them back to him.'

She didn't understand why he suddenly went quiet. Why his lips tightened so ominously. Why his eyes flashed, like lightning across the blackness of the cave sky.

'Ellis,' Morgan hissed. 'So he's in on this too? Is that what you were discussing, so cosily, at the café the other day? What is this – an insurance scam?'

Imogen stared at him dumbly. She felt exhausted. Utterly spent. 'I don't understand,' she murmured weakly.

'No? And I suppose you're not sleeping with him either?' he grated.

Imogen's eyes widened. 'Ellis?' she repeated blankly. 'Are you crazy? Ellis loves Averil.'

'And I love you,' he snarled. 'What's that got to do with anything?'

It was too much for her. She simply sat there, on the rock floor, staring up at him, surrounded by diamonds, coming totally unglued. For one wild moment there she'd thought she'd actually heard him say he loved her!

Something in Morgan finally gave way. A surrender so sweet he didn't even try to fight it. Instead, slowly, he sank to his knees in front of her. Holding her eyes with his own, he unzipped his wetsuit down to his navel and shrugged his shoulders out of it. It was cool in the cave, and she watched, bemused, as the goose flesh rose on his now bare arms.

Something inside her, as hot as lava, suddenly stirred. 'Morgan,' she whispered warningly.

He reached out and took the flat edge of her own zip between his fingers. He looked her in the eye. 'If you want to stop me,' he said softly, 'now's the time to do it.'

Imogen didn't move. Couldn't move. Slowly, the zip slid down. Her breasts quivered. Wordlessly, he leaned forward, sliding his hand underneath the rubber and cupping one of them in his hand. She wore no bra. She moaned as, beneath his rubbing thumb, one nipple burgeoned into life. And then she was lying on her back, staring up at the cave's ceiling. The torch rolled to one side, illuminating them in a narrow beam of light, highlighting one side of his face and hair in a white halo as his head slowly lowered over hers.

She saw the dark brown velvet of his eyes, the downward sweep of his drying hair, and then his lips were once again on hers. It was as if they'd been waiting for that moment forever.

She shuddered as he pushed the wetsuit down over her shoulders, exposing her all the way to her stomach, and gasped as his lips left hers, his head bent as his tongue dipped into her navel.

Compulsively, her legs jerked either side of him, and he kissed his way up her sternum. She felt the cool air on her breasts and gasped, then gasped again, louder, harsher, as his lips encased first her right, then her left nipple, his tongue flicking out and licking them until they throbbed with a dull and exquisite ache.

He moved from her for a few moments, and when he came back, as she knew he would, he was totally naked. She opened her eyes briefly, seeing in the torchlight the golden sheen of his skin stretched across taut muscles. Around them, the scattered diamonds shone like stars in a midnight sky. She lifted her hand to caress his shoulders, his arms, his chest, and her fingers encountered the silky-smooth touch of hair.

She closed her eyes for a moment, savouring the moment, and then opened them again as he lifted her and pulled the rubber from her completely. To accommodate him, she raised her hips from the rock and then she was free of the wetsuit and the shorts she'd worn underneath.

She moaned as his hands moved between her bare thighs. He kissed her again, then again, then again, all the while his hands exploring her body – the curve of her hips, the indentation of her waist, the globes of her breasts.

When one of his legs nudged hers apart, she was ready for him, the sensation of him filling her causing just one brief moment of pain – more exquisite than anything she'd thought possible.

His eyes shot open. 'Isadora,' he breathed, sounding humble and triumphant at the same time.

She said nothing, but gasped as he moved, as if to withdraw from her. But she needn't have worried. With a sure, slow stroke he thrust back into her, making her whole body convulse.

After that, her mind ceased to function as she was swept ever higher, ever further, until she was screaming his name uncontrollably, the sound of her voice ricocheting off the walls.

She didn't know it, but her nails gouged into his back as she arched and writhed beneath him. And soon, her cries of ecstasy were not the only ones to ricochet off the rock walls.

FIFTEEN

Ellis watched the yacht dock, and felt his heart sink as he recognised the woman on deck. Averil. Quickly he checked the name of the boat again, but there was no mistake. She'd been out on Tony Jackson's yacht.

He'd been waiting for the boat to return after finding out from another boat owner that Jackson had set sail late that morning. Who knew when Jackson might decide to try again, or even make a run for it?

Jackson himself came up on deck, and as Ellis watched with a heavy heart, Averil kissed Jackson demurely on the cheek and disembarked. Jackson watched her until she was out of sight, and then went below decks again. With a frown, Ellis set off after Averil, catching up with her just as she was about to unlock her car – a sporty little Corvette convertible.

'Hello. Did you have a nice time?' he asked, with just a touch of bite in his voice. Averil gasped and spun around.

'Ellis, don't sneak up on me like that,' she admonished, her eyes hungrily devouring him. He was wearing cut-off denims and a shirt so fine it was almost see-through.

'I saw you just get off Tony's boat,' he accused, unprepared to let it go, and Averil, still smarting about his intimate little get-together with Isadora Van Harte, shrugged nonchalantly.

'Tony? Yes, we had lunch together.' She unlocked her door and slipped in. 'It was just a friendly meal, nothing more,' she added meaningfully, shooting him a don't-you-dare-make-a-big-deal-of-this look.

'Fancy coming back to my place for a drink?' he asked softly, determined not to get into a fight with her about this.

'Only a drink?' she repeated softly, with a little moue of fake regret, her eyes sparkling.

His breath caught, and he laughed. 'All right. Something very cold – like lemonade stacked with ice cubes – followed by something very hot. I'll turn the air-conditioning right up. How does that sound?'

Averil laughed. 'It sounds wonderful. I'll follow you.'

'No need, I didn't bring the car. I travelled by bus.'

'How very noble of you,' Averil taunted. 'Scoot in then.'

Ellis scooted, and a few moments later they hit the road. At his condo he walked to the fridge and, as promised, filled two tall glasses with ice and lemonade. Averil watched him, sinking down onto a deep leather sofa and wondering how best to broach the subject of Isadora.

Although they'd only met a few times, she'd begun to think of Isadora as a friend – and had the feeling that they could become the best of friends, given time. It only made the whole thing all the more painful.

'Do you feel like dancing tonight?' Ellis asked, handing her her drink and letting his eyes wander over her. She'd sat with her legs – now bare of shoes – tucked under her, and her skirt had ridden high, showing a fine expanse of thigh. His eyes dropped to them with a glowing look.

Averil's breath caught. 'Dancing? Sure. Pick me up at nine.'

'All right. Cheers,' he reached down to clink glasses with her.

'Cheers,' Averil purred. They sipped, eyes locked. When she'd finished, she put her glass down deliberately, and leaned back against the soft leather. 'I thought you were going to put the air-conditioning up,' she murmured, and watched him as he did just that. 'Hm, it's not working,' she complained.

'Give it a chance, wo . . . man,' he gulped as Averil slowly began to undo her blouse buttons.

'Too slow,' she murmured with a sigh. 'I'm so hot I simply have to cool down somehow.'

Ellis watched her as she slipped out of the blouse and let it fall to the floor. Then she leaned back and stretched. 'Hmm, where's my drink?'

Wordlessly he knelt beside her and held his own glass to her lips. She sipped it, and then slowly ran her tongue across her lips. 'Ice?' she asked, holding out her hand.

'Uh-huh,' Ellis said gruffly, and hooking out a piece of ice, he slowly reached forward and held it about an inch from her sternum. One drop fell and she gasped, then smiled as he began to trace the ice cube across her skin, guiding it in ever increasing circles, right up to the lace of her bra. 'It's getting cold now,' he said, but his body was just beginning to burn.

Averil smiled and held out her arms. 'I'll warm you up,' she promised.

* * *

Miles away, in an underwater cave, Imogen was on her hands and knees, gathering up spilled diamonds. Morgan, feeling fluid and mellow, watched her as he got back into his diving suit.

In the summer they'd be able to dive without them, but even though the winter waters were relatively mild, he always preferred students and his diving instructors alike to don rubber. Just in case. Now he was almost too apathetic to struggle into the gear. He felt boneless and sleepy. Also replete and whole, for the first time in his life. And yet he knew they were in a mess. Just look at what the love of his life was doing, for pity's sake! Gathering up stolen gems.

'Can you see any more?' Imogen asked, shining the torch along the bottom of the flat rock where they'd just made love.

Her loins were throbbing and aching pleasantly. They said nothing about the fact that she'd just lost her virginity, although she was sure he knew. There would be time for that later, she hoped.

'No, I think that's all,' Morgan said crisply. 'Now, are you going to tell me what's going on?'

Imogen carefully kept her face averted so that he couldn't see the sudden pain in her eyes, and drew the suede bag tight. Wordlessly, she rewrapped it in the plastic bag, then tucked it very firmly into her diving belt. So much for hope, she thought bitterly. That Pandora really had a lot to answer for. Slowly, she looked up at Morgan, and then behind him, trying to harden her heart without much success.

'Later,' she said flatly. 'Let's get out of here first, before I lose my nerve. That underwater tunnel is . . .' She shuddered.

Morgan shook his head. 'You're crazy, do you know that? Diving on your own?' She raised contrite but unwavering blue eyes to his face, and he sighed.

'Come on then. Give me the torch and hold onto my hand. We'll go through together. It's just about wide enough.'

Imogen nodded wearily, and they clambered down the rock back to the ledge just above the sea. He turned twice to help her down, and both times his warm, firm, strong presence filled her with relief and confidence. In spite of everything, it was good to be no longer alone down here.

He helped her get into the tanks and checked them a second time, then donned his own gear. With a splash, they returned to the sea.

* * *

With the sweat cooling on his skin, Ellis got up and walked to the fridge to renew their drinks. As he did so, he noticed there was a voicemail message on his phone. He held it to his ear, eyes still on the naked, luscious figure on his couch.

Imogen's voice sounded tight and urgent, and Ellis felt himself stiffening. Something had happened! She must have found something out. Was she in danger from Tony? If Jackson ever discovered her true identity, her life wouldn't be worth tuppence. 'Damn,' he grunted, and hit the button to call the sender. Grace answered and told him that Elizabeth was in, but that Isadora had gone out sometime that afternoon. No, she hadn't said where. But Miss Isadora always informed them if she wouldn't be in for dinner, and she hadn't left any such message, so she should be returning soon.

Ellis thanked her and hung up. He was frowning hard by this time, and Averil, now dressed, watched his tense back with a feeling of fear churning in the pit of her stomach.

'Isadora?' she asked, trying to pick her way carefully through the minefield. She wanted to know the truth, and yet she dreaded it at the same time. If he ever said those dreaded words, 'there's someone else', she really felt as if she might die. It was that bad. That irrevocable. She swallowed hard.

'Yes. I've got to find her. But she's not at home.' His mind was working furiously. She couldn't have fallen foul of Jackson, surely, when not so long ago Averil had been on his boat. There hadn't been time. On the other hand, Imogen must have found out something important that related to her brother and the diamonds.

'Ellis?'

'Hm?'

'Are you in love with her?'

Ellis, naked and golden, spun around to stare at her. 'What?' He sounded so stunned that even Averil had to smile.

'You and Isadora,' she said tentatively. 'Morgan and I, we saw you and her together. At a little café near the harbour. You were holding hands and you looked so rapt.'

Ellis stared at her, appalled, and then shook his head as he realised how it must have looked. And how she must have been feeling these past forty-eight hours or so.

'Oh, Averil, no,' he said, walking towards her. 'No, no, it's nothing like that. That day you saw us, she'd just saved my life.'

'*What*?' she gasped, as he took her by her hands and led her back to the sofa.

There, he proceeded to tell her about the stolen gems, and his suspicions of Tony Jackson. With a tense tone and a fearful heart he admitted how he'd arranged to meet her in order to get the lowdown on her then boyfriend, and, when Averil made no angry or hurt demur, continued on quickly to describe the hit-and-run that had been no accident, and how it had shaken up Isadora and reminded her of the aeroplane tragedy.

'But that's not all,' he admitted. 'Isadora, it turns out, isn't really Isadora.' He was watching her closely, knowing he was breaking faith with Imogen, but trusting Averil with everything in him.

Averil's eyes widened. 'Not Isadora?' she whispered, trying to grapple with that concept, and thinking of Morgan.

Morgan who loved her.

'No. Her name is Imogen Dacres. And she's here because of her brother. Robbie.'

It took Averil a second to make the connection – to remember the death by 'accidental drowning' of one of her brother's divers. A diver called Robbie Dacres.

And then, as Ellis explained the rest of the story so far, things at last began to fall into place. Especially about their agreement to work together but concentrating on their own angles of investigation.

'So you think her phone message means she's found something out about her brother's death?' Averil asked, when he was finished.

'It sure sounded like it,' Ellis said, frowning once more. 'But she's not at home, and I don't like it. Not with Jackson on the loose.'

Averil suddenly sat upright, remembering the conversation she'd overheard just that morning. Quickly, she told him about it.

'It makes sense,' Ellis nodded a few moments later. '*Ice* is a common slang word for diamonds, and he'd have needed transportation to get them to wherever.'

'And the package at the airport he wanted collected must have been Isadora. No, Imogen,' Averil corrected herself, her eyes widening as she realised the full extent of her friend's danger. 'Oh, Ellis, no wonder she pretended to be Isadora! When those men came to the hospital looking for her, she must have been terrified. Morgan told me about it. He thought they were probably reporters but they weren't. And she must have known that. Just think – to come around in hospital after such an ordeal, only to find that there was another ordeal still ahead of you. I'd have been scared out of my wits.'

'Yes. She thought fast, and she's been clever and lucky so far,' Ellis agreed. 'But she's not out of the woods yet. None of us are. Not until we can find enough proof to get Tony Jackson convicted. Interpol would be ecstatic – they've been after him for years. I hate to tell you this, my love, but your ex-boyfriend is a crook on a major scale.'

'He wasn't really my boyfriend,' she denied at once. And then her eyes gleamed as she suddenly recalled a party on his yacht. Tony, who'd got a little drunk, had boasted to his guests about the boat's state-of-the-art safe. What had he said about it now . . .

'I think I'll get dressed and drive over to Elizabeth's,' Ellis interrupted her thoughts. 'See if Imogen's got back yet. I can't just sit here doing nothing.'

'Yes,' Averil agreed, eyes gleaming. 'You go.' She watched him lovingly as he dressed and searched for his car keys. Once he'd found them, he leaned down and kissed her. Hard. 'Wait here for me?' he murmured.

'All right,' Averil lied. For as soon as he'd gone, she knew just where she was going.

But first, she had to make a phone call.

* * *

Elizabeth looked up as Morgan and Imogen walked through into the main lounge. 'Morgan, how nice! You will stay for dinner, won't you?'

Morgan forced himself to smile at her gently. 'Thank you, Elizabeth, I think I will. But first, your niece and I have some things to discuss. You'll forgive us if we leave you for a few minutes?'

Elizabeth nodded, not missing the fact that he had Isadora's arm in a grip so tight that her skin was pale where his fingers dug in, or that, for whatever reason, Morgan was absolutely livid. She watched the two young people disappear, heading through the hall and towards Isadora's bedroom. She raised an eyebrow and wondered just how many fireworks were about to spark now. Really, she hadn't had so much fun in ages! She sighed with satisfaction, then leaned across to answer the telephone as it began to ring.

Pushing open her bedroom door, Morgan thrust Imogen cavalierly inside. 'Right, first of all, hand them over,' he said, in no mood now for tenderness.

After successfully getting back through the tunnel, returning the boat and gear to the diving school, and driving over here, he was determined to have an explanation. And his patience was fast wearing out.

For her part, Imogen was determined to remain silent. Morgan would go after Tony Jackson if she told him the truth, and knowing how dangerous that bastard was, she was determined to keep Morgan in the dark. Quite simply, what he didn't know couldn't hurt him. Even if it made him furious with her.

Outside, the doorbell rang, and Elizabeth, who'd just hung up the phone, sighed. Now what? It was certainly all go today. A few moments later, a beaming Grace showed Averil's good-looking Englishman into the room.

* * *

Averil parked her Corvette well away from the harbour and walked to the quay, aware of the slowly sinking sun and the tourists and beachcombers it brought out.

Careful to keep out of sight as much as possible, she spotted the *Sea Siren* tied up no more than a hundred yards away. At this time of night, most other boat owners were heading for the city's restaurants, and the quay looked reassuringly deserted. Noiselessly, she crossed the street and made her way towards Tony's yacht, looking around nervously as she did so.

She doubted that Tony would still be on board – he preferred the bright lights, people, noise and bustle of the big hotel restaurants to dining alone.

With her heart in her mouth, she crossed the gangplank and stepped on board. If she encountered any of the crew, she had her story all ready – a lost lipstick, in a Cartier gold and jewel-encrusted case which her mother had given her one birthday. Besides, the crew wouldn't be all that surprised or suspicious to see her back on board, especially since she *had* been out with them that morning and *might* have mislaid an expensive little trinket.

Nevertheless, her throat was dry as she tiptoed along the deck. She'd taken off her shoes for quietness, but even that she could explain away as not wanting to walk with high heels on the expensive wood decking.

As she reached the main salon, she glanced in quickly, relieved to see that it was empty. She slid open the doors, wincing at the slight noise they made, and walked down the few steps into the main living area. On the drive over, she'd remembered, all those months ago, what a drunken Tony had said about the safe.

'It's safe with the fishes,' he'd boasted drunkenly, and laughed himself sick. When she thought about Robbie Dacres dying, and his sister forced into hiding, and Ellis nearly being killed too . . . She took a deep breath, her heart hammering in her chest. Now was not the time to be a coward. Ellis and Imogen needed proof that Tony had received stolen goods, and she was damned well going to see if she could find it.

She looked around the room hopefully. If Tony was like 99 out of 100 of her acquaintances, the combination to his safe would probably consist of his birthday numbers. Anyway, it was worth a shot. Where would he keep anything incriminating?

But there was no fish tank cunningly hiding a safe. Or even a picture of fish. Damn! She bit her lip and wandered around, one ear cocked for the slightest sound, but there was nothing. She was about to give it up and see if it could be in the master bedroom when she saw his fishing trophy. It had been awarded to him when he'd caught a record swordfish before coming to Bermuda. He'd been so proud of it that he'd had it mounted on a marble plinth.

Grinning in anticipation, she made her way quickly to it, studying the gold and white trophy thoughtfully. She reached down and tugged on the curving moulded body of the fish, but without success. Squatting down in front of it, she studied it closely, then twisted the fish instead, and felt – with a jolt of excitement – it give way. With a gasp she began to lift the hinged lid off, and then froze.

'Averil, my sweet, I would hardly have classed you as a closet Raffles.'

She spun around, staring in dismay at Tony, who was standing in the doorway leading from the bedroom.

'What?' Averil asked weakly, her heart leaping into her throat and staying there, leaving her distressingly breathless.

Tony smiled – a hard, wide, shark-like smile which sent chills running down her spine. 'Raffles,' he repeated. 'The aristocratic gentleman thief.' And he looked pointedly at the exposed safe behind her. 'Don't tell me you're short of a dollar or two, sweetheart?'

Averil knew she should think of something, and quickly. Something witty, or even mildly plausible, something to divert his suspicion, but she just couldn't think of anything.

Tony sighed, and shook his head. 'Something tells me Bermuda isn't a particularly healthy place for me to be any more, Averil, my turtledove,' he said, still in that mock-sorrowful voice. As he walked towards her, she began to back away. 'I take it the new boyfriend has been blabbing?'

Averil swallowed hard, and felt her hip bump painfully into the corner of a secured bureau behind her. She flinched.

'I don't know what you mean, Tony,' she said, but even to her own ears it sounded woefully inadequate.

Tony shook his head, then made her jump as he suddenly shouted, 'Philippe. Philippe.' A moment later a steward looked in. 'Tell Olaf we're leaving now,' he gritted.

'Now, sir?' the steward said, obviously surprised. He glanced curiously at the pale-faced woman watching his boss with big, shocked brown eyes.

'Yes. Tell him to head north. We'll anchor for the night near that little island shaped like a half-moon. He'll know which one I mean. Then we sail at first light for Florida.'

'Yes, sir.' The steward backed away, sensing that something ugly was up, and that it would be best if he wasn't a witness to it.

'Florida?' Averil repeated nervously. 'Tony, I must get off. Now.' She tried to sound strong, to sound in charge, but she suspected she sounded more like a frightened little girl.

Tony obviously thought so, for he took a few steps to close the gap between them, and then reached to cup her chin in his fingers. Terrifyingly, he waggled her chin with mock-playfulness. Averil's breathing stopped for a horrendous moment. 'Oh, I don't think so, Averil,' he said softly, his voice like the sibilant hiss of a snake. 'I really don't think so. You can be my insurance.'

As she let out her breath in a near half-sob, he smiled again. 'Something tells me I might need it. And, when all's said and done, neither the boyfriend nor that brother of yours are going to risk you getting hurt. Are they, sweetheart?' he snarled, and with a vicious shove sent her sprawling.

SIXTEEN

Ellis knocked on the door and walked in, quickly aware that he'd entered a battle zone. Morgan and Imogen both swung their heads to face him, Morgan looking as black as thunder, Imogen stalwartly beleaguered.

'Hello, I got your message,' Ellis said firmly to Imogen. 'I was worried about you.' He turned to Morgan, who was looking positively cyclonic now. 'Morgan.'

'Reynolds,' Morgan said flatly, glaring.

Ellis raised an eyebrow. So he'd gone from Ellis to Reynolds had he? Now just how had he managed that?

Morgan saw the sardonic lift of his eyebrow and went into hurricane overdrive. 'Perhaps you'd care to tell me what the hell is going on?' he growled. 'I followed this, this *crazy woman*,' he hissed, pointing imperiously at Imogen, 'down an underwater cave system, when she's only had one lesson—' he began, then stopped abruptly as Ellis went pale and gaped at Imogen.

'You did what?' he yelped. 'Why didn't you wait for me?'

Morgan took a huge breath of air and slowly let it out. So, at least Isadora hadn't been lying when she'd said she and Ellis were working together.

'I had to. I figured the letter out,' Imogen said, getting flak from all sides now and not liking it one little bit.

Ellis blinked. 'The letter? There was something in it?'

Morgan, like a spectator at a tennis match, swung his head from Ellis to Imogen, then back again, checking strenuously for the least signs of intimacy between them. But he could find none, and that alone helped his temper slowly subside.

Imogen nodded, turning to Ellis now, her face bright. 'It was a silly code he made up when we were kids. That's why some of the words were written in a darker ink.'

Morgan suddenly realised they were talking about the letter he'd found in her jacket pocket the day he'd come snooping. 'Whose letter?' he gritted.

Imogen glanced at him, then at Ellis, and suddenly smiled widely. 'It told me where they were,' she said simply, still looking at Ellis, and then reached into Morgan's trouser pocket, where he'd placed the diamonds after taking them off her. The sensation of her hand against his thigh, her fingers scraping against his skin through the linen, had his body stirring in remembered pleasure. He gritted his teeth.

Ellis gaped as she withdrew the small suede bag. 'Here,' she said simply. 'Robbie must have taken them from wherever Tony put them, and hid them in the cave.'

Robbie? Morgan wondered. The 'R' in the letter. But . . .

Without a word, Ellis took the bag to a table and began to pour the sparkling stones onto the tabletop, counting them, assessing their colour and weight, and confirming that they were indeed his stones. 'You beauties,' Ellis crooned.

Imogen, fascinated, took a step towards the table, but felt a hand snake out and grab her arm, swinging her around. 'Start talking,' Morgan gritted. 'And now. I want the whole story, from the beginning, and it better be good.'

Imogen took one look into his eyes and knew when she was beaten. Simply, she told him. Everything. When she was finished, he stood staring at her, a series of expressions crossing his face as he took it all in.

'So you came here to avenge your brother,' he said at last. Of all the scenarios he'd thought of since learning she was an imposter, that had never been one of them.

'Yes. But it got so very complicated,' she said, appealing for his understanding. 'Mostly because of Tony Jackson's goons showing up at the hospital. It was then that I became Isadora . . .' She trailed off miserably.

She looked at him helplessly, not daring to think that he might forgive her for all the deceit, and worst of all, for suspecting him, at first, of being Robbie's killer. Her heart was in her eyes now, and he could see it plainly.

'So your name must be . . . Imogen,' Morgan said quietly. He slowly rolled the name around in his mind. Imogen. Im-o-gen. It was a beautiful name. It suited her so well. 'Imogen,' he said softly. 'I love you.'

Even Ellis, absorbed in his diamonds, shot his head up at that and took a quick look at them, then hastily began stowing the gems away. 'Er, I think I'd better . . .' He pointed to the door, but already Morgan was pulling the raven-haired beauty into his arms, and Ellis quickly scuttled away.

Outside, in the hall, he began to laugh. It was almost impossible to believe things could turn out so well. He walked back into the living room and started as Elizabeth looked up from her magazine. He'd almost forgotten where he was.

'Elizabeth,' he said softly, smiling. 'Have you ever seen what a quarter of a million pounds in loose diamonds look like?'

Elizabeth blinked. 'Er, no, I can't say I have.'

Ellis smiled and walked over to her, rattling the little bag in his hands. 'They look like this.'

In the bedroom, Morgan Dax carried Imogen Dacres to the bed.

* * *

In the locked guest bedroom on board the *Sea Siren,* Averil restlessly paced, trying to think of a way out. She checked the window again, but it was sealed shut. Without much hope, she picked up the big chunky glass ashtray, and once more rammed it into the glass, but the specially toughened window merely bounced the big ashtray back at her, making her shoulders and arms jolt painfully.

She dropped the ashtray on the thick-pile expensive white carpet and walked back to the door, yanking uselessly on it, then staring at it thoughtfully. What about picking the lock?

She hunted around for something to use, and then snapped her fingers. 'Coat hangers,' she muttered, running past the comfortable double bed to the built-in wardrobes and extracting a hanger. With a bit of twisting she managed to get one piece of wire straightened, and knelt down in front of the door, poking the sharp, stiff wire into the keyhole.

In a movie, of course, it would only take the heroine a few seconds to get the door open. Half an hour later, Averil gave up. The locks were obviously as state-of-the-art as everything else on this damned boat. She was almost crying with frustration. Every second, the boat was getting further and further away from Bermuda. From Ellis. From safety.

Because, as much as she tried to push the thought to one side, she didn't think she was going to be allowed to leave this boat alive. Giving way momentarily to despair and exhaustion, she sank onto the carpet, curling up in a foetal ball, and cried.

* * *

When Morgan and Imogen emerged from her room, Elizabeth was serving Ellis his second drink. 'Ah, there you are,' she said, pretending not to notice the melting looks on the two young lovers' faces. 'Ellis was just telling me all about his latest diamond buy. Wasn't it naughty of him to arrange to meet a seller here on the sly and not tell us about it?'

Ellis, Morgan and Imogen exchanged quick, knowing looks and silently agreed that it would be far kinder to Elizabeth to keep her in the dark.

'Ellis, dear, would you like to put those lovely gems of yours in my safe while we have dinner? You are staying to dinner, aren't you?' Elizabeth offered.

Ellis smiled and shook his head. 'I can't. I'm taking Averil dancing at . . .' he checked his watch and quickly stood up. 'Heck, not long from now! I better go home and get showered.'

'Averil?' Elizabeth said, obviously puzzled. 'Surely not. Are you sure you have the right night, Ellis?' Elizabeth waved a hand at the phone. 'It's just that she called me a while ago to say that she was going to Tony's yacht. She told me she was going to come here afterwards for a nightcap and asked me to call you, Ellis dear, if she hadn't arrived by ten. To tell you she'd been delayed on the *Sea Siren*.'

Ellis stared at the old woman, his face totally draining of colour, then looked at Morgan, who'd gone similarly pale. Imogen grasped his arm hard. 'Morgan,' she said urgently. 'Elizabeth, we have to go,' she said hurriedly to the old lady, who watched all three rush out with a grim look in her eyes.

It was going to be a long night by the look of it, Elizabeth thought, and reached stalwartly for the bottle of port.

* * *

In the master bedroom, Tony Jackson went through the list of things he had to do. Transfer all his money from the Bermudan banks. Sell his house – through dummy corporations of course. Change his identity again. Something French this time perhaps. He knew a man in Marseilles who did a great line in forged papers. He drank off the last of his champagne and leaned back, rubbing his eyes tiredly. The world was a big place, with plenty of playgrounds for a man such as himself. Fiji next, maybe. Or the Seychelles.

He got up and walked through the narrow corridor, pausing by Averil's door, hearing muted sobs coming from within. He smiled grimly. 'Too late for tears now, sweetheart,' he murmured viciously. If she'd played her cards right, she could have been Mrs Tony Jackson. But no, she had to go snooping. He shook his head and moved on to the dining room, where his chef had prepared lobster bisque, followed by smoked salmon with capers and a light and frothy zabaglione for dessert.

He hated to perform tiresome tasks on an empty stomach.

'Philippe, how long before we anchor for the night?'

'Another hour yet, sir,' the steward informed him. 'There's a storm warning for later tonight, and the captain says we have to be careful about sand banks.'

'Yes, yes, all right,' Tony snarled. 'I didn't ask for a weather report.'

In her room, Averil got up and began to check the hinges on the door. If she couldn't unpick the lock, perhaps she could unscrew the hinges. Quite what she'd do after that she didn't know, but she'd cross that bridge when she came to it. *If* she came to it.

* * *

'Where are we going?' Ellis yelled, as they all piled into Morgan's Jaguar – Imogen, perforce, having to sit on his lap.

'The diving school,' Morgan gritted, turning on the engine and skidding away from the house, going up the gears and pressing the speedometer needle hard. 'I've got a speedboat there, and I'd bet this year's turnover that he's already well underway.'

Ellis watched the speedometer rise to nearly ninety, and wished it would go even faster. Imogen was sure they'd attract the attention of the police, and welcomed it. They might need their help before long.

'I'll kill her,' Ellis muttered under his breath. 'Of all the scatter-brained, idiotic things to do.'

'Don't tell me about the craziness of women,' Morgan muttered, shooting Imogen a speaking glance. He too felt sick to his stomach with worry about his sister. After hearing that Jackson had murdered Robbie Dacres, he didn't even want to think about her being on his boat. 'What time is it?'

'Nearly nine,' Ellis said curtly.

They managed to arrive at the harbour without attracting the attention of a policeman, and it only took them a moment to see that Jackson's yacht was not in dock. Morgan ran to the office, opening up and going straight for the radio. Quickly he put out a general message, asking any boats out there if they'd seen the *Sea Siren* that evening.

Ellis came running in. 'They put out to sea nearly an hour ago,' he panted, having asked around.

Morgan held out a hand, staring at the radio intently. Within a few moments, it crackled into life. Morgan Dax had a lot of friends on the high seas.

* * *

Tony finished his meal as the steady throbbing of the engines suddenly ceased. They must be there. He went up on deck, looking out at the small island shaped like a C that was spread out before him. He sipped his cognac and stared at the moon, thinking back to the first time he'd met Averil. How he'd always been given a kiss at her door with not even an invitation in for coffee. Now he began to wonder, not for the first time of course, what it would be like to have sex with Averil Dax.

And smiled as he realised that there was nothing to stop him finding out. Now.

* * *

Imogen clung on to the side of the boat for dear life. Both men had tried to insist she stay behind at the office, but she wasn't having any of that. Besides, she'd pointed out, once they'd rescued Averil, she might need a woman friend. This had sobered them both right up, and she'd watched, grim but unprotesting, as Morgan extracted two big diving knives from the equipment cupboard and wordlessly handed one over to Ellis. Ellis had taken it, weighing it in his hand, testing the grip, then nodded and tucked it into his belt in the small of his back.

After that, everything had become something of a blur. Breaking the speed limits in the harbour, Morgan set the boat hammering out, heading north-west. A small pleasure craft had told them they'd spotted the *Sea Siren* not ten minutes before, heading past them towards the furthermost reaches of the islands. After that, it was open ocean all the way to the American south-eastern seaboard. But since there was a storm warning out, nobody in their right mind would do anything but anchor up in a sheltered bay for the night.

Now, as the speedboat engine roared and bounced them over the night ocean, Imogen clung on, her stomach doing flip-flops every time the speedboat bounced over a wave. She sent silent messages across the ocean.

Hold on, Averil. Just hold on. We're coming.

Sitting on the passenger seat beside Morgan, Ellis stared straight ahead. He'd never felt so scared or so frustrated in all his life. But there was nothing he could do. He glanced at Morgan's set profile, watching him squeeze the maximum out of the boat, gaining miles and time with every passing moment, and fought off the blinding anger which threatened to overwhelm him. He had to keep a clear head.

Let her be all right. Ellis closed his eyes in despair, and prayed like he'd never prayed before. *Let her be all right. Let her be all right.*

* * *

Averil jumped as the key turned in the lock and she shot up off her knees, where she'd been endeavouring to unscrew the bottom hinge with the coat hanger.

The door opened and Tony filled the doorway, stepping inside and smiling at her. 'Averil. You don't look too hot, old thing. You haven't been crying have you?'

Averil backed away slowly, the wire hanger hidden behind her back. 'Tony, this is silly,' she said, her voice little more than a croak. 'Why don't you just—'

'Ah-ah-ah,' Tony said, waving a finger at her, and Averil suddenly realised that he was drunk. She didn't know whether to be relieved or not. Drunk men were always so unpredictable.

'You don't tell me what to do anymore, sweetheart,' Tony warned her, leaning back on the door and smiling at her savagely. 'The days when you led Tony Jackson around like a bull with a ring through his nose are well and truly gone.' He spaced his words out ominously, and Averil felt her heart sink.

Fear, hot and sharp, tasted like iron in her throat.

* * *

'Ellis, do you know how to use radar?' Morgan asked, as, out of the bright, moonlit night he began to come upon the series of small, uninhabited islands. He knew Jackson's captain vaguely – the Swede had a reputation as a careful man, and he wouldn't take a yacht out at night when a storm was forecast. That meant they must be anchored up somewhere.

'Sure, I think so,' Ellis said, curiously. 'Why?'

'I want you to turn it on and see if you can find any craft anchored out here among these islands,' Morgan said.

He slowly powered the boat down, and Imogen felt safe enough to unclasp her stiff fingers from the side of the boat. She duck-walked forward as Ellis turned on the radar and began to scan the green screen, his eyes already scanning hard. *Averil, Averil, where are you?* 'There,' he said quickly. 'There's a small craft to the east of here.'

Morgan slowed the boat to a near-stop and risked leaving the wheel to look. 'Too small,' he said at once. 'Jackson's yacht is a much bigger baby altogether.' He returned to the wheel and began to steer the boat through the channels, searching for the tell-tale white gleam of a boat's hull in the bright moonlight. Soon the storm clouds would form, and there'd be no chance of seeing them with the naked eye.

Ellis began to sweat. What if they weren't here at all, but heading straight for Florida?

* * *

Averil slowly backed away from Tony, trying to stop herself from getting hysterical. Now was definitely not the time to panic. Even so, it was hard. Rape was not something you ever thought could happen to you. It was something you read about in the papers, or heard had happened to a friend of a friend. And yet, here and now, right in this incongruously luxurious yacht's bedroom, she could feel its ugly dark threat.

'Tony, don't you think you've had too much to drink?' she asked, trying to sound as non-judgemental as she could. She kept backing away, her fingers flexing spasmodically around the coat hanger. As a weapon it seemed so flimsy and puny, but it was the only thing she'd got. 'Things will look so different in the morning,' she coaxed.

Tony smiled. 'Oh, I agree,' he said, making hope flair briefly within her heart, only to be dashed with his next words. 'In the morning, I'll have spent the night with you,' he smiled savagely. 'Oh, but don't look so worried, *cara mia*,' he purred. 'I'll be a much better lover than that milk-and-water Englishman of yours, I promise. Didn't anyone ever tell you,' he suddenly snarled, launching himself across the room at her, 'that Latin lovers are the best!'

* * *

'That looks bigger,' Ellis said, pointing to another solid green wedge on the radar. 'Near that crescent-moon-shaped island.'

Again Morgan powered the boat down and checked it. 'Let's take a look,' he said briefly, and turned the speedboat, with a lurch, towards the island.

* * *

Averil cried out and fell backwards, whipping her hand out and jabbing blindly with the piece of wire. It caught him squarely on his upper arm, gouging out a line of flesh, and with a yell of surprise and an incredulous look at the blood suddenly forming on his arm, Tony staggered back.

Averil continued to back away. *The door!* her brain suddenly screamed at her. He didn't lock the door after coming in. If only she could get around him and to it, she could at least get out of this room. But would his crew help her? Surely Captain Olaf would! If she could only get to him, she was sure he'd protect her.

'You bitch,' Tony snarled, and let rip a torrent of abusive Italian, and with a cry of despair, Averil made a dash for it.

* * *

'That's her,' Morgan hissed, powering his way towards the yacht.

Ellis felt his mind and body leap with a powerful sense of elation. Averil! 'Hold on, girl, we're coming,' he whispered with grim determination.

On the deck of the yacht, several members of the cabin crew heard the speedboat long before they saw it. When it came powering out of the moonlit night at them, they simply watched it come, mouths agape.

With a rough bump, Morgan brought their craft level with the boat, and Ellis leapt for the boarding ladder before Morgan had even switched off the engine. He swarmed up the ladder and jumped on deck, turning a menacing face at the first man he saw. 'Where is she?' he snarled.

The steward, Philippe, looked at the angry blond-haired Englishman in front of him, wondering what to do. Tony Jackson was not a man to be crossed easily. 'Hey? Who—?' he said, feigning ignorance. And then he saw Morgan Dax appear above the railings and haul himself on board, and he began to look truly scared.

'My sister's on board this boat,' Morgan gritted, glancing beyond Philippe to the men who were slowly gathering behind him. 'The police know we are here, and will be coming shortly,' he lied with utter conviction. 'If anything's happened to my sister, you'll be the sorriest bunch of bastards ever to—'

'She's down below, Mr Dax, sir,' Philippe said quickly. 'In the guest bedroom.'

Ellis turned first, diving into the lounge and looking around.

'There,' Morgan pointed forward, and Ellis ran down the narrow set of stairs like a greyhound, Morgan right behind him.

* * *

Averil felt herself bounce as she was thrown onto the bed, her eyes wide with fear as Tony fell on top of her. She hit out blindly, raking his face with her nails, screaming at the top of her lungs.

Ellis, who was making for the wrong bedroom, heard her blood-curdling screams and went cold and skidded to a halt. Morgan, now in the best position behind him, turned and got to the origin of the screaming first, bursting through the door like a fury. He saw his sister on the bed, twisting and screaming beneath Tony, whose hand was raised to punch her.

With a yell, Morgan reached forward and literally hauled him off her, yanking him backwards. Behind him Ellis appeared and, as Morgan swung the stunned Italian around, the blond-haired Englishman threw him a massive punch that buried into Tony's stomach. Jackson screamed and bent over, retching.

Ellis caught him another punch under his chin, and Jackson fell like sack of potatoes onto the floor, unconscious.

Averil, stunned by the sudden events, stared first at her brother, then beyond him to Ellis. Mutely, she held out her arms and Ellis rushed to her, gathering her against his chest, holding her tightly, rocking her back and forth.

'If he's touched you, I'll kill him,' he said, and meant it. 'Darling, it's over. I'm here.' He kissed her hair feverishly, rubbing her back with his hands in a timeless gesture of comfort.

Morgan glanced at Jackson's crumpled form and sneered, then slowly backed out of the room. With charges of kidnapping and attempted rape to add to the list, Jackson would be an old man before he ever got out of prison. Morgan would see to *that*.

Above him, Imogen started to come down the stairs. Quickly, he moved to intercept her, smiling an answer to her worried, questioning look. Averil wouldn't be needing her tonight.

Back in the cabin, Averil sobbed tears of relief and joy, and raised her face to Ellis to be kissed. 'I'm all right,' she murmured, over and over again, comforting him now as much as being comforted herself.

Now that she was in his arms again, nothing else mattered.

SEVENTEEN

Imogen looked up nervously as Morgan walked in, meeting his eyes questioningly. She was sitting on the sofa in Elizabeth's favourite lounge, feeling sick with nerves.

As Morgan stood slightly to one side, the ginger-haired figure of Giles, Elizabeth's doctor, was immediately visible.

It was January. Christmas had come and gone, with Averil announcing her engagement to Ellis and Morgan his to Imogen. Elizabeth had been in a frenzy of pleasurable delight ever since, overseeing the 'double wedding of the century', as she insisted on calling it.

And certainly Bermuda's high society was rising to the challenge. The ceremony was to be held on the beach below Olympus, and wedding organisers had been frantically coming up with ideas and themes in an attempt to win the commission, Elizabeth ruling them with a surprising rod of iron.

Trellises, to be draped with live roses, were in the process of being made. Yards and yards of white carpet had been laid out in various patterns on the beach, lifted up and laid again, to get the best effect. The island's florists were on red alert.

The island's top ladies had been jetting off to Milan, New York, London and Paris in order to buy their outfits.

Family jewels were being buffed and polished even as Imogen rose and smiled at the doctor tremulously.

'I've already told him,' Morgan said at once, and Imogen smiled and looked at the ginger-haired man nervously.

'I suppose you're mad at me?' she asked quietly.

Giles looked at his ex-patient thoughtfully, unaware that Imogen was holding her breath, then slowly shook his head. 'No. No, I can't say I blame you really,' he finally replied.

The arrest and trial of Tony Jackson had been a sensation in Bermuda for the last two months. The man's brutality and conviction for the murder of Robbie Dacres, the kidnap and attempted rape of Averil Dax, not to mention the other charges, had appalled everyone who'd ever sat down at the same dinner table with him.

Averil had had to keep a very low profile for a while, but the reporters had now left, and her life was getting back to something like normal. She and Ellis planned to honeymoon in Iceland (one of the few places Ellis could discover that she'd never been), and then they would be making their home in Antwerp. Averil was already eagerly house-hunting online.

Morgan and Imogen, of course, were going to be staying in Bermuda, with Imogen moving into his house by the sea. But first, she'd insisted, they had to be married.

And it had been one cosy evening as she, Morgan, Averil and Ellis were discussing their weddings that Imogen had suddenly clapped a hand to her mouth and looked stricken.

Everyone had looked at her in alarm, and when she'd told them what she'd suddenly realised, they all understood her predicament at once.

For she could hardly stand up in church, so to speak, and answer to the name of Isadora Van Harte. And, since Elizabeth would be in the congregation, she could hardly answer to her real name of Imogen Dacres either.

At least, not without telling her 'aunt' first.

Which was why Morgan had arranged for this lunch at Hartelands, with the doctor in attendance.

'Elizabeth is just getting changed,' Imogen said, offering the doctor the seat beside her. 'Have you brought everything you might need?' she asked, looking down at the medical bag in his hand with a cold shiver. What if Elizabeth collapsed and . . . No. She mustn't think about that.

Giles nodded. 'Yes,' he said grimly.

Imogen flushed guiltily. 'I know,' she said sadly. 'You don't need to tell me. But at the time, I was so scared . . .' she trailed off as Morgan reached for her hand and squeezed it encouragingly.

'Oh, I know that,' Giles tried to reassure her. 'From what we've learned of Tony Jackson, you almost certainly saved your own life by your quick thinking. You mustn't think that I blame—' He hastily broke off as the door opened and Elizabeth walked in.

They were in the big lounge facing the gardens with the hummingbird feeder, and the light poured into the pleasant ivory and gold room. Elizabeth, leaning on her cane, was dressed in a white outfit of flared trousers and a short-sleeved lacy blouse. A row of pearls hung in smug pink-white glowing balls around her neck.

'Giles, so glad you could come,' Elizabeth said, walking forward and offering her cheek for its usual peck. 'Drinks?'

Eventually, when they were all seated with glasses of fruit punch, Elizabeth glanced from the carefully blank-faced Morgan to Imogen, who couldn't quite meet her eyes, to the scrutinising gaze of her doctor. 'So,' Elizabeth said placidly. 'What's going on?'

Imogen wasn't really surprised by Elizabeth's intuition. Over the months she'd come to learn that very little escaped her 'aunt'. She looked at Morgan nervously.

'Well, Elizabeth, it's like this,' Morgan began, leaning forward in his chair and watching her nervously. 'We've got something rather upsetting to tell you.'

'It's all my fault,' Imogen blurted out, wringing her hands. Elizabeth turned her calm brown gaze towards Imogen and smiled. Her eyes were probing.

'I see,' she mused. 'Am I going to learn who you truly are at last?' she added mildly.

Imogen stared at her. Beside her, Giles smothered an exclamation. Only Morgan carried on looking at her steadily. 'You're a wise old bird, aren't you?' he said finally, affectionately.

Elizabeth looked at him with twinkling eyes. 'Impudence,' she said, but she was beginning to smile.

'B-but, I don't understand,' Imogen stuttered into life again. 'Are you saying you know that I'm not . . . not . . .'

'Isadora?' Elizabeth helped her out gently. 'Of course I know that,' she said, almost dismissively. 'I've known that ever since I first saw you at the hospital.'

Giles stiffened. 'You never said,' he accused suddenly. 'It must have come as a real shock to you. You must have felt ill,' he growled. 'Why didn't you say something?'

Elizabeth sighed and sipped her drink thoughtfully, amused to be the centre of so much attention again. 'Well, you see, it was obvious to me that the young lady,' here she looked at Imogen with a smile, 'was in some kind of a jam. And she was obviously very frightened indeed when those two oafs pushed their way into the room. I must say, I didn't like the look of them at all myself. So when she pretended to be Isadora, and deliberately called me "aunt", I decided that she was probably being very sensible, and played along with her. Besides, she'd just been through such a terrible ordeal. It wouldn't have been Christian not to help her.'

Imogen's mouth fell open. Morgan simply looked at the remarkable old lady and shook his head. 'And what if it had turned out that the reason she was in a jam was because she was a criminal or something? A drug smuggler perhaps, and those two men had been customs?'

'Oh really, Morgan, have some sense,' Elizabeth said reprovingly. 'If they'd been police they'd have said so. Besides, if it had turned out that my house guest was, well, less than savoury shall we say, of course I would have called in the police. But it only took me a few days to realise she was perfectly wonderful.' Elizabeth beamed at Imogen, who realised she was gaping like a guppy and suddenly shut her jaw shut with a snap.

Beside her, Giles cleared his throat. 'How do you feel now, Elizabeth?' he asked calmly.

'Fine,' the redoubtable old lady shot back. 'Just curious. What is your real name, my dear? It wouldn't be Imogen Dacres by any chance, would it?'

Morgan began to laugh. Elizabeth looked at him knowingly, as at a fellow conspirator.

'Well, I happened to remember that that was the name of the person those two horrid gentlemen were looking for, so it seemed a reasonable bet,' she explained defensively.

'Now you know why I never play cards with her,' Morgan said to Giles, who was also smiling and shaking his head.

'But, Elizabeth,' Imogen gasped. 'How did you know I wasn't Isadora?'

'Oh, I knew that after one look at you, my dear,' Elizabeth said.

'But on the flight over, when I was talking to the real Isadora, she gave me the impression that you'd never met, let alone exchanged photographs,' Imogen protested.

'Oh, we hadn't,' Elizabeth agreed. 'And you don't need to tiptoe around me, my dear, like you're afraid to speak her name. I've now come to terms with the fact that I lost my only niece to that dreadful accident. So many of the bodies were never recovered, you know. And, in a strange way, that helped. It was as if the sea simply took her before she ever reached me, and that was how it was meant to be.' She shrugged sadly.

Wordlessly, Imogen reached out and took Elizabeth's hand in her own. She squeezed it gently. 'We sat next to each other on the plane. Isadora was a lovely woman, I could tell that immediately,' she said softly. 'And she was so pleased to be coming to meet you. She told me how glad she was to have the chance to heal a family rift.'

Elizabeth's eyes misted slightly. 'Thank you, Imogen,' she said firmly. 'I know you're being honest with me.' Imogen nodded.

'Come on, Elizabeth, give,' Morgan interrupted, knowing how much the old lady hated any show of morbidity. To prove him right, Elizabeth leaned back, letting Imogen's hand go, and took a sip of her drink.

'Just how did you know we had an imposter on our hands?' Morgan demanded.

Elizabeth took another sip of her iced drink, deliberately and mischievously letting the moment drag, then, giving in to all the appealing looks being sent her way, relented and said, 'It's simple. It was her eyes.'

'My eyes?' Imogen repeated blankly.

'Yes. Both my brother and his wife had brown eyes,' Elizabeth said simply. 'Our parents did too, and I believe his wife's parents also. So, with the rules of genetics being what they are, I thought it very unlikely that they should produce a blue-eyed child.'

Imogen began to laugh. She couldn't help it. All this time she'd been so guilty about lying to Elizabeth, when all the time she hadn't been fooling her for one moment.

And it served her right!

Suddenly Morgan was laughing too, and then Elizabeth, and then Giles. When Grace came in to announce that lunch was ready, she found them all laughing like loons.

* * *

February the fourteenth, Valentine's day, dawned with a perfect Bermudan sunrise. From the terrace of Olympus, Averil and Morgan looked down onto the private beach, watching as the small army of people set about establishing the site of their weddings.

The whole Dax clan had descended from the States during the course of the previous week, with Morgan and Averil's parents seeming delighted with Ellis and Imogen.

‘Isn’t it strange?’ Averil murmured, as two men, struggling to carry a huge container of trailing roses, headed for the archway of white trellises being set up by hammering workmen. ‘Watching them down there, knowing that in . . .’ she checked her watch, ‘just three hours’ time we’ll be down there getting married?’

Morgan laughed softly. ‘You’re telling me,’ he said. And holding out his arm, he pulled Averil against him and looped a hand around her shoulder. For a long while, brother and sister stared down onto the white sand below.

* * *

Two and a half hours later, the last of the guests were assembled on the rows of chairs. The white carpet was in place. The roses had been wound through the arches. The organist and his instrument were all set.

The vicar, clad in white robes which were being blown around his legs by a playful sea breeze, stood waiting, his knowing eyes checking out the two nervous men before him.

Both were in traditional grey silk wedding suits. Ellis glanced across at Morgan and raised an eyebrow.

‘Scared stiff,’ Morgan whispered back. Ellis grinned. At least he wasn’t the only one!

And then the smile faded as the organist suddenly broke into the wedding march. As one, the congregation turned to watch the two women approaching, and gave a collective gasp of appreciation.

Averil, on the arm of her proud, Pouter pigeon of a father, was wearing a white taffeta tea dress with a boat-shaped neckline, showing off her honey-tanned skin to perfection. A short veil covered her face, blowing against her in the breeze. Beneath it, her hair, coiffed and held in place by a diamond tiara (her husband’s gift to her), glowed like wheat in a summer’s field. She carried a huge bouquet of bird-of-paradise flowers.

Ellis caught his breath, his green eyes glittering like peridots as she smiled at him from beneath the veil. A little to one side of him, Justin stood ready as his best man with a sparkling diamond ring in his breast pocket, the finest cut and carat that Reynolds-Smythe could find.

Morgan had eyes only for the woman by his sister's side. Imogen's own absentee father had been contacted and now walked by her side, not quite sure what to make of it all. Despite his limited presence in her life, he'd been shocked to the core to hear of her death in a tragic plane crash, especially so soon after his son Robbie's diving accident. Then to learn that not only was she alive but was getting married – and that his son had in fact been murdered, and Imogen had tracked the bastard down – it was almost more than the man could cope with. But nonetheless he was here, and was determined to play his part in this most special of days.

Imogen was dressed in a full white wedding gown with long sleeves and a high neck, a long train flowing behind her.

Both women had agreed that they wanted to look as individual as possible. Grace and Elizabeth walked behind Imogen, holding the train and then letting it fall in an arranged swathe before taking their seats.

Unlike Averil, she'd opted to do without a veil, and her dark raven hair made a startling contrast to the white gown. Held back in the most elegant of French pleats, orange blossoms were woven into its midnight richness. She was carrying a small posy of blue flowers. As she walked up to stand beside Morgan, her eyes were bluer than the ocean.

The vicar couldn't remember ever marrying more handsome couples. In their chairs, Elizabeth and Grace reached simultaneously for their hankies. The organist fell silent. Four full hearts looked to the vicar, ready to take their vows to love and honour forever and ever.

Over their heads a single gull wheeled and cried as the vicar began to speak.

THE END

ALSO BY FAITH MARTIN

DI HILLARY GREENE SERIES
Book 1: MURDER ON THE OXFORD CANAL
Book 2: MURDER AT THE UNIVERSITY
Book 3: MURDER OF THE BRIDE
Book 4: MURDER IN THE VILLAGE
Book 5: MURDER IN THE FAMILY
Book 6: MURDER AT HOME
Book 7: MURDER IN THE MEADOW
Book 8: MURDER IN THE MANSION
Book 9: MURDER IN THE GARDEN
Book 10: MURDER BY FIRE
Book 11: MURDER AT WORK
Book 12: MURDER NEVER RETIRES
Book 13: MURDER OF A LOVER
Book 14: MURDER NEVER MISSES
Book 15: MURDER AT MIDNIGHT
Book 16: MURDER IN MIND
Book 17: HILLARY'S FINAL CASE
Book 18: HILLARY'S BACK

JENNY STARLING MYSTERIES
Book 1: THE BIRTHDAY MYSTERY
Book 2: THE WINTER MYSTERY
Book 3: THE RIVERBOAT MYSTERY
Book 4: THE CASTLE MYSTERY
Book 5: THE OXFORD MYSTERY
Book 6: THE TEATIME MYSTERY
Book 7: THE COUNTRY INN MYSTERY

MONICA NOBLE MYSTERIES
Book 1: THE VICARAGE MURDER
Book 2: THE FLOWER SHOW MURDER
Book 3: THE MANOR HOUSE MURDER

GREAT READS

THE LYING GAME
AN OXFORD REVENGE AN
OXFORD SCANDAL AN
OXFORD ENEMY
AN OXFORD SECRET
AN OXFORD FRAUD
AN OXFORD TRIAL
AN OXFORD INHERITANCE
AN OXFORD SUSPECT
IMPOSTERS IN PARADISE

Thank you for reading this book.

If you enjoyed it please leave feedback on Amazon or Goodreads, and if there is anything we missed or you have a question about, then please get in touch. We appreciate you choosing our book.

Founded in 2014 in Shoreditch, London, we at Joffe Books pride ourselves on our history of innovative publishing. We were thrilled to be shortlisted for Independent Publisher of the Year at the British Book Awards.

www.joffebooks.com

We're very grateful to eagle-eyed readers who take the time to contact us. Please send any errors you find to corrections@joffebooks.com. We'll get them fixed ASAP.

Printed in Great Britain
by Amazon

61883922R00121